IF I WAS YOUR BEST FRIEND

A Novella

LUCINDA JOHN

Shan Presents, LLC

If I Was Your Best Friend

Copyright © 2018 by Lucinda John

Published by Shan Presents
www.shanpresents.com

SUBSCRIBE

Text Shan to 22828 to stay up to date with new releases, sneak peeks, contest, and more....

WANT TO BE A PART OF SHAN PRESENTS?

To submit your manuscript to Shan Presents, please send the first three chapters and synopsis to submissions@shanpresents.com

Chapter One

YSSA

"**D**amn, my nigga, you see that bitch? Got damn that ass moving in them shorts! Aye redbone! Lemme holla at you right quick." Rolling my eyes, I let out a hard sigh as I pushed my way through the crowd of niggas that loitered the front of the store, ignoring the blatant outburst from the rude ass scrub dressed in all black.

Glancing over at him, I took note that he was ok looking, in between fine and ugly. Although he was rough looking with a slew of nappy dreads bunched up in a thick ponytail at the top of his head, he had potential. Gazing down at his feet, I turned my nose up and continued my stride into the store. The dusty ass Nike slide that he rocked with a pair of worn out crew socks sealed his fate with me. He wasn't worth my precious time. That nigga was broke and a broke nigga couldn't do shit for me.

Winking at Abdul, the owner of the convenience store son, I made a beeline to the back of the store where the coolers where located. The moment I swung open the glass door the cool air rushed me giving me that breeze I desperately needed dealing with Florida's hot ass sun. Today it was in the high nineties, my entire body was covered in sweat due to me walking the damn block.

"You good over there?" A tall caramel, medium built, Shemar Moore look-a-like brother asked as he sized me up.

Taking in his neatly shaved bald head, the small diamonds he wore in each ear, the Rolex that looked as if it could keep every dairy product in this store cool for days, I decided to play into his little game. I was three hundred dollars short on my rent, and quickly calculating the designer threads that adorned his sexy frame, I knew without a doubt I could make my rent money and have more money left over. The solid gold wedding band he wore on his ring finger was a turn-off; however, I was in no mood for standards. I needed the money today and I was willing to do just about anything, if the price was right.

"You need something out of here?" I asked licking my lips.

"You got something over there for me?" He flirted back.

"Hmmm." I stared off to space as if I was toying with my thoughts. "You wanna come take a look and see?" My tone challenging him.

Shifting all of my weight to my left leg, I slightly turned my body to the right giving him a clear view of my ass cheeks that dipped out from the bottom of the denim skinny jeans that I skillfully cut into a pair of coochie cutters. The blue fabric was tight and snug against my one hundred-and-forty-five pound frame drawing attention to my apple booty and pussy print.

"Damn." He hissed before invading my personal space. "Hand me a Corona." His soft plush lips grazed my ears while the soft breeze from his minty breath caused the hairs on my back to stand up.

"Here you go." I smirked handing him two.

"Get anything else you want." He uttered, his voice was laced with lust.

"Say no more." I turned on the heels of my brown Old Navy slides that matched the one size small tank top I wore tied into a knot underneath my breasts, displaying my pink shiny belly ring.

Purposely swinging my young hips in circular motions, I made my way to the shelf that were decorated with potato chips. Running my fingers across the various bags, I grabbed two Salt and Vinegar, cheddar flavored Ruffles, a bag of white cheddar popcorn and two bags of Hot Fries. With an arm filled with chips, I dropped them on the counter before making my way to the end cap covered with cookies grabbing two bags of Grandma Cookies. At the counter, I unscrewed the top of the Hot Sausage jar and fished through it for the end piece before placing it in a sandwich. Shemar Moore's look-a-like busied himself on his phone unfazed by the fact that I was racking up the snacks.

"I'm done." I smiled, placing two pickled eggs that was nice and pink from soaking in the Hot Sausage juice down next to four packs of Mamba's, Airheads, and peanut flavored M&M's and the big bottle of Strawberry Ritz soda. The countered was covered with various snacks but as if it was nothing he paid the bill with a crisp hundred dollar bill ordering Abdul to give me the change.

Bingo!

I smiled on the inside; this brother had bread and he was down with spending it. All I had to do was turn up the sexy, with a bit of charm and my rent for the month was as good as paid.

"I know your little ass ain't about to eat all of that?" He questioned the moment we were out of the store.

"Try me." I chuckled.

I may have been little but I had the appetite of a grown ass man. Since I didn't have a car and spent most of my days walking I easily burned off all the calories I would consume throughout the day.

"What you about to get into?" He questioned as he made his way to a clean all white Audi.

Following him, I replied, "Nothing." The tone of my voice was filled with excitement thinking of all the possibilities.

"Take a ride with me then." He offered.

"What's your name?" I rebutted.

"D Rock but you can call me D."

"That's what your mama named you?" My brows connected as I furrowed them.

"Nah but that's what you can call me." His thick pink tongue swiped against his beautiful pink lips. "What about you?"

"I'm Yssa, pronounced, E-SUH!" I hated when people mis-pronounced my name; therefore, I made it my business to give the proper pronunciation before anyone had the chance to rub me the wrong way by butchering it.

"All right then, E-SUH!" He mocked me. "You riding with me or what?"

"I'll ride." I shrugged.

The thought of ditching the heat for a car blasting with cool air caused my mouth to water. I was hoping that D was prepared to give me what I needed so I could go home to take a nice, long shower before rolling up a nice spliff and indulging in my two bags filled with snacks.

"You smoke?" He asked the moment he started up the car.

"Yes." A smile graced my face as I reclined my seat back, kicked off my sandals and crossed my pretty feet against the dash.

"Alright, I'mma swing by my man's house and grab some fiya, then we gon ride."

"That's fine with me." I closed my eyes enjoying the breeze from the A.C.

Midway through our drive to his weed man's house, his phone started ringing off the hook. He ignored the first three calls but when they kept coming in, he sucked in a deep breath, forcefully letting it out before snatching up his BlackBerry and answering.

"Yo!" the sexiness of his voice soothed me as I continued to enjoy our ride.

"Damien, where you at?" A woman's voice snapped.

I was unfazed by his conversation but that didn't stop me from ear hustling.

"I'm with Bruno man; we handling business." D Rock, D, Damien... whoever he wanted to call himself snapped.

"Today was supposed to be your day off! I thought we was supposed to be packing up for our trip to the Bahamas." The caller, who I was willing to bet was his wife, mouthed off.

"Come on, man, you called me with that rah-rah shit. You really need me to help you pack?" He growled.

"Excuse me for wanting your opinion on a few outfits before I packed them up." She sucked her teeth.

"How about this, don't pack shit, I'll take you shopping and you can buy brand new everything." D reasoned.

"I like the sound of that." She beamed.

Just like that her high pitch tone had now dropped down to a sweet coo. He had wooed her with a shopping trip. Hell, if I was her I would have dropped my attitude too. There was nothing wrong with some brand new threads to rock on a trip out the country.

"I'm so excited to be celebrating our first year of marriage together on the beach sipping Bahama Mama's." I could hear the smile in her voice and she serenaded how much she loved him.

"Let me get this money and I'mma holla at you later." Was his response before he hung up the phone.

Chuckling a little too loud I kept my eyes closed praying he was too engrossed in driving to have heard me.

"What's so funny?" He asked.

"Nothing." I shrugged, my eyes still closed.

"I'm married." He cleared the air.

"I knew that the minute I sized you up." I responded.

"Just clearing it up."

"Listen, I'm just tryna chill and come up on some money to pay the rest of my rent. I have bills and you have a wife; we both have our personal issues." I looked over at him.

"How much?"

"A band." The amount rolled off my tongue before my mind could register what I was saying. I knew he had money but I wasn't sure if he was trying to trick off that much. The last thing I needed was to mess up this little connect, forcing me back on the streets waiting on John's to respond to my Back- Page ad.

"Two bands if you take this ride with me."

"You're willing to pay me two thousand dollars to take a ride with you?"

"Yup." He shrugged. "I'm too fly to trick off for some pussy." He chuckled.

"I'm down!" I relaxed, grateful that I would be two thousand dollars richer, without having to give a little ass to get there.

Entering the city of Port St. Lucie, which was two hours away from my home in Fort Lauderdale, when D said he wanted to ride, I didn't think he meant go on a mission. The moment we pulled into the middle class neighborhood, driving past beautiful brick family homes decorated with luscious green grass and bright colored flowers my mouth began to drool in anticipation for the *fiya* D was about to cop. The weed had to be good as fuck if he drove two hours to get it.

"This nigga be wilding." D huffed throwing the car in park in front of a beautiful brown house with a stucco finish. The house was everything. Although, the other houses on the block looked equally nice, this one in particular stood out like a sore thumb. The house alone gave the house a more lavished feel, boosting the neighborhood's value.

Out front was a couple that looked out of place, arguing. The woman who was one of those little people, voice could be heard loud and clear as she argued with the dude that stood about 5'7. Despite the fact that she looked as if she was 4'9 her voiced carried through the entire block vibrating D's tinted windows as she stood on a chair with her fingers in the dude's face trying to get her point across.

Bringing my hands to my lips, I tried my best to stifle the laugh that threatened to escape my lips. The entire scene was comical as fuck. The dude's handsome face was twisted into a deep scowl as he stood there chest rapidly rising and falling while he puffed on a blunt in attempt to calm his nerves. Without warning, as if she was Superman or some shit, Lil Mama leaped out of the chair and jumped on buddy attacking him.

"These motherfuckers always on that fuck shit." D mumbled to himself as he swung open the driver's side door and rushed over to the arguing pair.

"No, she didn't." I chuckled. Clutching my stomach, I doubled over laughing my ass off as I watched D try to pry Lil Mama off of the dude. Her small fist were bawled up tight as she wind milled them around connecting a few shots, missing some.

"This bitch is mental I swear!" Dude yelled once D was able to successfully separate them.

"Nah D, this nigga keep trying to play me." She growled jumping around from side to side looking like a hyperactive toddler.

"Man, take yo ass in the house before I kick your small ass over." D growled.

"Fuck y'all." She sucked her teeth before storming into the house, tripping over the chair she was standing on in the process.

"What the fuck." I howled out as tears trickled down my face from how hard I was laughing.

D rushed the dude, a sexy brother who looked biracial, and if I had to guess, was mixed between African American and Puerto Rican, into the house. His beautiful hair that was once concealed by a rubber-band that held it in a low ponytail was now wild and all over the place. I waited in the car playing with the thread that were now left behind from when I cut up my jeans while popping a piece of Trident Gum.

A few minutes later all three of them walked out of the house and walked towards the car. D got in the driver's seat while the other two go in the back.

"That's my hommie Block and this his girl Noya." D introduced the crazy couple.

"Hey girl." Noya waved at me.

"Wassup?" I replied looking over at her.

Noya was very pretty, her butterscotch skin matched her hazel eyes perfectly. She was thick as fuck too. She had more cakes than Debbie as she sat there looking like a mini stripper. The pair looked so odd together but completed each other at the same time. Block and Noya had one of those opposite attracts type of relationships.

D drove up a few more blocks before he pulled in front of another house, this one not as lavished as the one before. D and Block both got out of the car and entered the house.

"You got another piece of gum?" Noya asked me.

"Uh-huh." I replied handing her a pack so she could get one.

"I didn't do well with females. I barely had any friends so her making conversation with me was a bit awkward.

"You fucking with D like that?" She questioned popping her gum.

"Nah." I kept my answer short. I didn't know who the fuck she was or who she was affiliated with. The last thing I needed was this itty bitty bitch fucking with my cash flow. I was here to ride, collect my money and go home.

"When D and Block returned, I watched as they placed a few bags in the truck of a Honda that was in a driveway and the rest into the truck of the Toyota that was parked next to it. Block got in the passenger's seat of the Toyota while D walked back to the car.

"Come on ma." He spoke causing me to look up at him.

He must have sensed my hesitation because he pulled out a knot of money and tossed it into my lap.

"All I want you to do is ride, but first I need you to change into this." He said handing me a bag that was in his hand.

A look of confusion plastered my face as I looked from him to the small bag.

"You wanna make this money right?" He questioned in a hushed tone.

Nodding my head, I got out of the car, grabbed the bag and went into the house so I could change my clothes. The bathroom was creepy as fuck. The entire back wall was covered in mirrors; the person who must have lived was a bit conceited because this was entirely too many mirrors for a bathroom. Pealing the clothes from my body, I faced the mirrored walls, giving my naked frame a look over. I was slender with a flat stomach, narrow hips, B-cup perky breasts, toned legs and a big ass. My golden colored complexion was blemish-free with the exception of the tramp stamp I had on my back. Yssa was tattooed in huge, neat cursive lettering above my ass with a colorful butterfly sitting at the top of the letter "A". My name was the only thing in this world that I had; it was the only thing I had to identify myself by, and the meaning of my name alone made me feel like someone, which was why I took offense when someone butchered it.

"Great." I sighed as I stood there staring at my reflection dressed in a KFC uniform.

Taking out the knot D handed me, I made sure the bathroom door was locked before I laid the bills out on the counter and started counting them.

"Twenty-five hundred dollars, damn." I beamed putting the bills in chronological order from the smallest to the largest.

"You good in there?" A knock at the door interrupted my thoughts.

"Yes." I breathed out before creating two stacked and placing one in each breast. Pushing the door open, I was greeted by D's handsome face while he sized me up.

"Alright, let's go."

Walking out the house behind D we got in the Honda and pulled off. Block, Noya and the Toyota was already gone. In silence, we drove until we arrived to a truck stop.

"You know how to drive?" D asked me.

"Yeah."

"You got your license."

"Yup." I lied.

I never got around to taking the driving test but I had my restricts due to a driver's ed course I passed in school.

"Good, I want you to take over driving from here for me; a nigga is tired as fuck. All you gotta do is follow the GPS." He tossed me the keys. "Let's get something to eat first." D suggested.

Walking into the truck stop, I settled for something light, a turkey club sandwich while he feasted on food from Panda Express and Burger King. We ate in silence, well I was the silent one while D ran his mouth on the phone the entire time. I could tell he was an unfaithful hoe ass nigga; this fool had mad bitches and he made time to talk to them all in the short period of time we spent at the truck stop.

Behind the wheel of the car, I cancelled out everything as I focused on the road.

"Don't speed." He ordered.

Easing my feet off the gas, I kept a steady pace as I drove allowing the voice of the GPS to lead the way; a few hours later we were entering the projects in the city of Jacksonville.

"Drive around the block three times before pulling up in front of the warehouse."

Doing as I was told, I drove around the block three times then pulled in front of the warehouse where there was a black sedan waiting with two big buff dudes standing next to it. My heart began to pound uncontrollably, my palms glided off the steering wheel due to the sweat that was starting to form all over due to me being nervous.

"Get out and walk to the stop sign. Block is going to pick you up and bring you back to the hotel." D spoke.

"The hotel?" I stuttered.

"Ain't no funny shit. I just need you from around here while I handle some business. I'mma bring you back home once I get done." He assured me.

Against my better judgement, I got out of the car and walked to the stop sign as I was instructed. A few minutes later, Block pulled up in a Suzuki.

"This your first time huh?" Block chuckled as I got in the car.

"First time doing what?" I questioned.

"Transporting."

"Transporting?" I side-eyed his ass.

"What the fuck else you thought you was doing. You just drove around with twenty keys of coke in the trunk." Block informed me. I started to feel sick thinking the amount of time I could have done if I would of gotten caught.

"Is there anything in this car?" I asked.

"Nah. How old are you?"

"Twenty- one." I lied.

He didn't need to know my business as long as he knew I was old enough.

"Cool."

"Where your girl at?" I asked.

"She handling business." Was his only response as he drove me to the hotel.

"Here you go." He handed me a room key. "You can order room service if you want. D will be back later on to drop you home." He winked before pulling off.

Locating the room by the number that was plastered on the back of the keycard, I walked inside of the room and made my way to the bathroom. Stripping out of the KFC uniform, I removed my panties and bra and tossed them into the washer along with my shorts and tank top. Making my way to the bathroom, I adjusted the dials of the shower until the water was nice and hot before getting in. Since my slayed slick press was sweating out I decided to wash my hair, until each strand coiled back into its natural state.

With a towel wrapped around my hair, I slipped into the hotel robe that hung on the back of the door, before sinking my body into the plush sheets.

"Damn I wish I had my bag of snacks." I huffed. I was agitated as fuck. All I wanted to do was smoke, eat my snacks and make a couple of dollars to complete my rent; all this other shit was extra and overrated.

✌

"You good?" D woke me up from my nap. Looking over at the clock it was almost midnight.

"Yeah. Let me put my clothes in the dryer right quick and we can go." I stretched.

"Brush your teeth too." He joked.

"Shut up." I playfully punched him before walking over to the laundry area. Once my clothes were in the washer I brushed my teeth, washed my face and my coochie before returning to where D was seated rolling a blunt.

"Thank God." I called out causing him to laugh.

"Good looking out on today." He spoke as he sprinkled weed into the center of the Dutch. I watched as he added wrap to it. "This shit makes the weed burn smoother." He spoke as if he was answering my thoughts.

"It's all good. I made my money for my bills so it's all good." I shrugged.

"You good huh?" He quizzed firing up the blunt.

"Yeah, I'm good." My legs bounced in anticipation. The weed was potent, intoxicating, but the way D pulled on the spliff I was sure it was fiya.

"Here." He handed it to me.

Taking the blunt between my manicured fingers, I sucked on the end, inhaling deeply before tossing my head back and allowing the fumes to take control of my body.

"This is good." I choked out.

"You handling that shit like a pro tho." He chuckled.

"These some grown woman lungs." I chuckled taking another toke before passing the blunt back.

Two blunts later and the room was thick with smoke. A box of pizza sat in the middle of us as we chomped down on the oozing cheesy goodness. Each slice I consumed felt like heaven. I had the munchies and this cheese pizza was everything to me. On a normal day I hated pizza but at a time like this I was more than willing to eat an unbutchered cow to ease my hunger.

"Where your man at?" D opened back up our line of communication.

"If I had one I wouldn't be here right now."

"Make sense." He licked his lips. The look of lust returned. My middle began to tingle as the suspense of what was going to happen next began to overwhelm me.

"Take that robe off; let me see something."

"You gotta pay to play." I licked my lips.

"Damn, I ain't pay you enough."

"That was for me to transport for you; this is something different." I smacked my lips. Even though I would willingly give D the pussy, I knew better. D had a wife. I'd be a fool to let him fuck on me, leaving me behind with a pussy pumped with lies while he returned home to his wife. I needed something in return. I wanted some bread.

"I don't trick off on pussy but..." His word got caught in his throat when I slightly rose my legs in the air, teasing him with a glimpse of my pussy.

"Damn." He sucked in a deep breath. "How much?" A groan escaped his lips as if he regretted the words.

"Another two grands." I pushed my luck. For leverage, I opened my legs wide open and began toying with my clitoris.

"Damn, alright." He stood and began removing his clothes. When his boxers fell to the floor so did my mouth. D was hung like a horse. My center began drip at the sight of his perfectly sized dick. The mushroom tip oozed out pre-come as I stood to my feet allowing the rode to fall to my feet.

"That pussy is fat." He groaned, massaging the veins that entwined around his shaft.

"Bring that shit over here ma." He huffed.

Doing as I was told, I made my way over to him. Roughly, D pushed me on the middle of the bed flipping me over until I laid flat on my stomach. The sound of him shuffling through his pants pocket for a condom had me on edge. My body began to shiver in anticipation as I impatiently waited for him to roll the condom over his juicy meat before entering me.

"Ouuuuuu!" I called out as he filled my girth.

"Damn this pussy biting." He huffed.

Hiking my ass high in the air, while pressing down on my back, D stroked my middle with nice slow stroke pacing himself so that he wouldn't come prematurely. Once he was able to gain his composure, D picked up the pace and began ramming his dick in and out of slapping my ass hard with every stroke.

"Ohhhh slow down!" I called out.

"Nah stop running, take this dick, all of it!" He ordered.

Re-adjusting my hips, I grabbed a hold of the bed post and started throwing my ass back at him, clenching my pussy around his dick, choking the life out of it with every grind of my hips.

"Stop doing that shit!" He growled clawing at my ass cheeks.

"Take this pussy." I taunted as I continued to fuck him until he spoke in tongues.

I may have been young but I was experienced in the sex department; it was my specialty, it was how I survived amongst other things. I was a wild child, I lived a wild life, I had no direction so I did what I had to, to survive. The struggle taught me a lot and at this moment I was using some of those tricks on D as I fucked him senselessly.

"Fuck girl, damn." He groaned. I could feel his dick swelling up in me alerting me that he was near his climax. Reaching between my legs, I toyed with my clit while sucking his dick in, trapping him in my slippery hole.

D sucked in a deep breath, his movements began to slow down, my pussy was slowly draining him as it milked his dick dry.

"Fuck." I aspirated falling on me causing me to collapse on the bed.

"I ain't gonna front; you got some good pussy." He complimented me, while using his right hand to play in my center.

"Mmmm." I moaned as my body responded to his touch.

"I wanna taste it." He spoke before lowering his head between my legs.

"Ahhh damn D!" Fisting the sheets, I arched my back forcing my pussy in his mouth. As if he had been deprived from food, D feasted on my goodies as if he was on death row and this was his last meal. My kitty purred, as it dripped like a leaking faucet. Lapping up every single drop, D pressed his mouth into my center shaking his head from side to side, the friction alone was enough for me to erupt.

The way he alternated between tongue fucking me and sucking my clit had my legs shaking. A few seconds later, I was struggling to breathe after an earth-shattering orgasm ripped through my body temporarily paralyzing me.

"I'm ready for round two." He spoke, wiping my juices away from his lips with the back of his hand.

Just as he was rolling the condom off his dick to replace it with a new one, the room clicked, the door knob twisted, and a woman barged in. D's eyes grew as wide as saucers, and I could already predict how everything was going to play out. This was his wife and she was about to start a fucking scene. Rolling my eyes, I reached for the rubber-band that was on my wrist and tied my hair up, preparing myself to fight, if I had to.

"What the fuck Damien!" She shrieked. Reaching for the lamp that sat on the table she threw it at him missing him.

"Chill out Diane man." He walked over to her dick swinging, wet with his cum.

"You really in this bitch fucking another girl and you telling me to chill out!" She yelled, enraged by what was going on.

While she shouted as he attempted to restrain her, I walked over to the dryer and rapidly put my clothes on. I made sure I had all my money, this time rolling it up and placing it in my pocket. I couldn't risk putting it in my bra and losing it if I had to rumble with Diane.

"Bitch, you one nasty ass hoe!" She shouted at me. "He's fucking married hoe, you see his ring! He's married." She shouted at me.

I wanted to sympathize with her, I felt bad, but I needed the money. At that moment, I came first, she didn't know me, she had no right to judge me. I stood off to the side with my mouth shut. D wasn't my man so there was no purpose in adding fuel to this fire by engaging in a shouting match with her. All I wanted to do at this point was collect the two grand he owed me in exchange for the twat I gave him.

"Man c'mon Diane, let's go." D had her hoisted in the corner, putting all his weight on her while he attempted to re-dress using one hand.

"Fuck you Damien! Fuck you! Why you protecting that hoe?!" She fumed.

"I'm not protecting that hoe. I'm just not trying to get you locked up behind some shit. These folks done already called the laws so it's only a matter of time. Come on ma." He tugged on her waist.

"How could you hurt me like this." She broke down in his arms crying.

"To be honest, I don't even remember what happened. I was fucked up. I know that's not an excuse but a nigga was really rolling. Had I been sober, this would have never happened." He lied. D may have been high but he wasn't rolling on shit; however, it wasn't my business so I kept my mouth shut.

"I'm sorry." He continued to plead with her until she finally gave in and left with him.

"I hope you ain't pay for this room." She fussed." If you did I want that hoe out, now!"

"Nah, you know me better than that, ma. I don't trick my money on hoes." He lied again.

Once they were gone, I gathered my things, snatched up the rest of the weed and left the room. It was about 3am, my phone was on 1% and I had no idea on how to get the fuck back home. I contemplated getting another room just to be on the safe side, but at seventeen I was sure no one at the front desk would check me in. With no other choice, I went back into the hotel room, and sat by the door, with a butter knife in my hand. I had to be prepared if Diane decided to come back or send one of her homegirls out here.

With a blanket thrown over my body, I sat in a chair with my back against the door and decided to get some rest. I was still tight about D bitch ass not paying me my other two grand; I was so pissed that I ended up falling asleep.

At about seven in the morning, I woke up with a bad crook in my neck from sleeping in the chair. Walking to the bathroom, I brushed my teeth, washed my face, and prepared myself for the task of getting back home. Just as I was preparing to walk out the door, a knock startled me. Grabbing the knife, I walked to the door, ready for whatever.

Through the peephole, I spotted Block. Although he was D's friend, I didn't know how he was going to approach me so I kept the knife clutched in my left hand while I swung the door open with my right.

"What the fuck you about to do with that?" He chuckled.

"You never know when you may need to protect yourself."

"D told me about what happened. That shit wild man. My fault, I have a feeling Noya ass said something; she real cool with Diane's sister." Block explained.

"No biggie. D send you with something for me?" I asked propping my right hand on my hip. I needed my money and I needed it now.

"Yeah." He laughed reaching in his pocket and pulling out a knot. "He told me to bring you home too, you ready."

"Yeah." I replied.

"Five G's, that pussy must be good for my boy to break that much bread."

"You tryna find out?" I challenged.

"I mean, shit." Block licked his lips.

"I got three bands on me right now tho." He sized me up and down.

Pushing the door closed, I pulled him over to the chair I previously slept in. I kept my seductive glare on him as I unbuckled his pants and covered his dick with one of the condoms D left behind. Once his dick was hard and secured, I dropped my pants and panties to the ground, propped my legs on each end of the chair, and rode his dick in reverse cowgirl.

Chapter Two

YSSA

Beep! Beep! Beep! Beep!
The blaring sound of my alarm clock sounded through my bedroom causing a loud groan to escape my lips. I'd just slipped in bed from my adventurous weekend with D Rock and Block four hours ago, physically I wasn't ready to get up yet. Sucking in a deep breath, I kicked my lime green and purple comforter off my body before wiggling my feet into a pair of house slippers. Exhaling, I stretched my arms, stood to my feet then stretched the rest of my body.

Walking through the small space of my box sized bedroom, I reached under my twin sized bed for one of my suitcases. It was a rip-off renting out this small ass room for five hundred dollars a month that didn't come with a closet. The tiny walk-in closet that was attached to the room was *off limits* since the broad I was renting this room from used it as a storage space for her child's belongings. As much As I wanted to bitch and moan about not being able to properly store hang my clothes in hangers, I held my tongue. Prior to this, I was homeless and because I was a minor, this was my only option. Even though my living arrangement was tight I was still grateful, a bed was a bed.

Fumbling with the coordinates, I popped open the lock that

secured my belongings and began rummaging through the pile of neatly folded clothes for something to wear. Iesha, the woman I was renting this room from, would find every excuse to walk in and out of my room which was why I kept my things locked. Once I had my clothes and toiletries in tow, I secured the lock on my things and made my way to the door. Cracking the door open, I searched up and down the hallway before running into the bathroom, shutting then locking the door behind me.

Twisting the dial, I prayed that there was enough hot water to shower in. Between everyone that ran in and out of this house, I was lucky if I was able to get the water warm enough to tolerate. Applying an ample amount of toothpaste to my toothbrush, I brushed my teeth, rinsed, gargled with Listerine then rinsed again. Curving my lips into a wide smile, I was immediately satisfied with every single one of my thirty-two, perfectly white teeth that flashed back at me. Pealing my clothes from my body, I got in the shower, enjoying the way the hot water penetrated my sore skin. Slipping a pair of bath gloves on my hands, I pumped a large amount of Olay body wash in the palm of my hands, rubbed them together, then lathered my entire body before rinsing off the suds.

After my shower, I dried my body and got dressed in the bathroom. With no time to spare, I brushed the front of my hair with some Pro-Style black gel, then placed a headband around my wild curly coils. I hated when my hair was in its natural state, but I had no choice but to rock it this way. Content with how I looked in my black, white, and red jersey dress, I slipped my feet into a pair of white strappy sandals, wrapping the strings up my thigh then tying them into bows just above my knees.

Racing back to my room, I quickly placed everything where they belonged before performing a final walkthrough of my room making sure the bed was made and everything else was neatly back in place. I hated living in filth. Iesha would allow her kids to run wild and mess up the things that were in the closet in my room without bothering to clean up behind them. It frustrated me to see their mess, but because I had this phobia I often found myself cleaning up behind her nasty ass and her kids.

"Good morning girl, you got the rent money?" Iesha sung.

"Yup." I replied reaching in my purse and handing her one thousand dollars. "This is for rent this month and next." I spoke looking her in the eyes.

Iesha was a very pretty girl; she was cool too but not cool enough for me to consider a friend. I didn't have friends, not because I couldn't make any but because I couldn't tolerate these bitches. Being around Iesha and females that I went to school with taught me that these hoes could not be trusted. The only reason I was cordial with Iesha was because she took me in even though I was a stranger.

Five months ago, I was living with my foster mom, Katie, whom I've been living with since I was fifteen. Although her household wasn't the best, it was the most stable one I've been in. From the moment my caseworker delivered me to Katie, her brother, Ron, began lusting over me. As time went on his advances became more frequent. He went from visiting once a week for Sunday dinner to finding every excuse to come over. One night, Ron was over playing cards with Katie's husband and his friends, he got so drunk that he had to crash on the couch. That night he entered my bedroom, pinned me down and robbed me of my virginity.

When I confided in Katie about it, instead of reprimanding her brother, she looked me in the eyes and asked me what I got out of it. She told me that pussy should not be free whether it was taken involuntarily or consented. For a second, I was confused, dumbfounded that she would say this to me, a minor that the state trusted to be in her care, but when she called her brother over and demanded that he pay me for raping me I knew she was serious.

With time, I got used to it. Instead of thinking it was rape, I looked at it as my job. Katie would turn a blind eye when her twenty-five-year old brother would sneak into my room and have his way with me. He even had some of his clothes in a duffle bag under my bed. At fifteen, I was in a forced relationship with a man ten years older than me and every adult in that household saw nothing wrong with it. I thought about reporting this to my caseworker but when Katie explained to me that things could get much worse, I kept my mouth closed and adapted to the behavior I was being taught.

Word of mouth had Katie's husband curious because he wanted a piece of the pie too. Shortly after, my foster *father* and I began our secret affair. He paid me more than Ron and sex was a lot more enjoyable with him. With two grown men sexing me up and leaving money by my bedside, I learned at an early age that pussy came with a price.

The day that Katie's husband called out of work was the day Katie came home from work early and caught us in the act. She was furious. We fought for hours until it was decided that I had to go. Katie promised not to report me as long as I stayed out of her house, and in return, I blackmailed her into breaking me off two-hundred dollars a month for my silence. I wasn't dumb. I knew I was getting a check from the state every month, a check that Katie money hungry ass wasn't ready to give up.

"You don't hear me talking to you?" Iesha asked snapping me out of my thoughts.

"Wassup?" I licked my lips.

"I said you must have hit a real lick to be able to pay two months of rent." She smacked her lips, reaching for her box of Newport's.

"Something like that." I inwardly rolled my eyes at the roaches that were climbing out of the sink that was piled with dirty dishes."

Nasty ass bitch, I thought to myself as my skin began to crawl. I could feel myself having a panic attack being associated with such filth. Scanning the kitchen, I searched for a broom and a mop. When I didn't see one, I made a mental note to gift her nasty ass one along with some cleaning supplies.

"Esh, where my boxers at?" Tony, Iesha's pimp, asked as he walked up on us smacking me hard on the ass.

I didn't miss the disapproving look Iesha gave me; it was a look I was all too familiar with. I didn't want Ron, but she didn't seem to think so. Every time he would come around disrespecting her by feeling up on me she would do little things to me out of spite. I didn't have time for the madness today. I had no choice but to go to school. Katie called me fussing that if I didn't go, the caseworker would drop by, and I didn't want to deal with the drama that would come soon after the home visit; therefore, I decided I would go to school, sit in the back of all my classes and catch up on some much-needed sleep.

"When you gonna come work for me, Red?" Tony questioned, allowing his eyes to roam freely all over my body.

"That girl is not interested." Iesha waved him off.

She was right, I wasn't. I had no desire to be somebody's bottom bitch. I had sex for money when I needed to. I didn't need anyone dictating my pussy then stealing all of my hard-earned cash. Iesha's room was like a revolving door with the plethora of Johns she had running in and out of her room. Her twat sold like hotcakes yet she lived in a roach-infested, low-income house in the projects with nothing but a thirty-day bus card to her name. Tony ceased every single dollar she made. In his mind, she didn't need money. He paid her three hundred dollars rent, her food stamps provided her with food, anything extra she had to ask permission to have. That wasn't the life I was trying to live.

"Shut the fuck up Esh!" He barked. "She can speak for herself..." he dropped the menacing glare he was giving Iesha and smiled at me. "You want to work for daddy. I'll take real good care of you Red, just say the word." His foul smelling breath penetrated my nostrils causing my face to contort into a scowl.

"I'm good." I stepped back. I needed a few feet to breathe. I was dying from the odor that seeped from his gums, polluting the air.

"You good." He grunted. "You think you too good for me or something?"

"Matter fact I do." Rolling my eyes, I turned on my heels, "Iesha, I'll catch up with you later." I shook my head before walking off.

"Stupid ass hoe!" He screamed halting my steps.

Looking back at him, I chuckled, "Nah being a stupid hoe would be me allowing you to pimp my pussy leaving me with nothing but a wet ass. I may be a young hoe, but a stupid one? Nah." I tossed over my shoulders.

"Bitch, I will fuck you up!" Tony rushed over to me grabbing me by my shoulder blades.

"Hit me and I will call the cops on you!" I threatened.

Tony's eyes turned into slits as he eyes me with so much malice in his heart. Tightening his grip on my shoulder blades he squeezed them until a sharp pain rushed up my spine.

"I'll break yo shit!" Shaking me, Tony tossed me to the ground forcing my head to hit the tile floor with a loud thud.

"Fuck you!" I squealed, scrambling to my feet and running out of the house. "FUCK!!!" I shouted when the bus I needed to take flew past me.

Reaching for my phone, I called up a cab and waited for the driver to arrive. Plopping down on the bus bench, I rolled my shoulders in a circular motion trying to relieve some of the pain.

 ❧

Sitting in the back of my last period math class staring at the red second hand on the clock tic away, I anticipated the sound of the lunch bell. The drama that transpired that morning forced me to skip out on breakfast, and it was a decision I regretted. I doubled over in pain as the aches from being hungry consumed my body. I was prepared to walk out of Mr. Hart's boring ass explanation of the equation he scribbled on the board, one that I had already mentally solved the minute it was written; however, I was trying to steer clear of getting into any more trouble. I was already hanging on by a thread, the only reason I was still holding on was because of my academics. I barely came to school let alone paid attention in class but I had the ability to pass all of my assignments with flying colors. The teachers hated me but the school benefited from my high test scores.

Brrrrrrrrrring!

The bell forced me to my feet.

"I dismiss my class not the bell." Mr. Hart called out but it was already too late.

With my things in my hand, I rushed my way to the cafeteria trying to avoid the traffic of students I would have to fight my way through. Walking over to the hot lunch line, I purchased a double cheeseburger, wings, fries and a bottle of water before taking a seat at one of the benches located in the senior patio. I didn't really care about the patio or being a senior. I just needed a place to sit that would shield me from the sun while I smashed down on my food.

The hoot and hollering from the students filled the air as the cheerleaders made their way to the patio. Today they were raising money for the senior breakfast, another activity I had no plans on attending. Bopping my head to Ludacris, *How Low*, I cleaned my chicken bones while occasionally gazing up at the cheerleaders while they performed. Once they were done, the football players walked around with flyers for their annual school dance.

"Here you go sexy." A voice caused me to look up from my burger.

"I'm not interested." I waved him off. I hated when people from school conversated with me.

"Why not?" He asked.

Sizing up the football player rocking the navy blue and white upper classmen leather men jacket, I couldn't deny the fact that he was sexy. His skin was a smooth butterscotch complexion. The braids that decorated his head was zigzagged to perfection, and whoever braided his hair took their time perfecting every cornrow. Mr. Football player's teeth was nice and white, he was tall, built and he smelled good; nonetheless he was sexy but I still wasn't interested in this dance.

"It's not my thing." I shrugged.

"Make it your thing. I wanna see you there." He flirted, sizing me up and down.

"Oh yeah? Why is that?" I flirted back. Reaching for one of my napkins, I cleaned my hands before reaching in my bag for a bottle of hand sanitizer.

"You fine as fuck that's why." He whispered. Giving me a whiff of his cologne. It was rare that you encountered a nice smelling jock in high school. I was surprised he smelled like something other than sweat and raw feet.

"What the fuck is this Bobby?" A cheerleader interrupted us. Bobby looked up at her, but I paid the broad no mind. Grabbing my bottle of water, I took a sip while examining my nails.

"Come on, Kerri, man chill." He pleaded.

"Why you over here in some girl's face Bobby? Why you playing me?"

"Ain't nobody playing you. I was just inviting her to the dance." Bobby explained.

Chuckling, I shook my head.

"Something funny hoe?" Kerri turned her attention to me.

"You talking to me?" I quizzed, licking my lips.

"Nah the hoe behind you, yes I'm talking to you!" She confirmed.

"Bobby, getcha girl, I'm chilling man."

"Nah don't say shit to her; direct everything to me."

"Kerri let's go, man, you tripping." Bobby tried to diffuse the situation.

"Nah fuck her." She knocked over the tray of chicken bones in my lap.

Licking my lips, I stood to my feet, reached around Bobby who was now trying to restrain her and popped her ass right in the face.

"Stop sizing me hoe!" I fumed.

"Oh no! Did this hoe just hit me?"

"I sure did!" I spat.

Furry surged through my body as I stood in my fighting stance ready to throw blows if I had to.

"What's going on over here?" The security guard asked fighting through the crowd that had now formed around the three of us. Some of the students had their phones trained on us, anticipating a fight so they could record it.

"Mr. Jones, she hit me!" Kerri cried, further pissing me off.

If I was going to get suspended for hitting Kerri I was going to make the suspension worth it. While everyone's guard was down, I rushed Kerri knocking her to her feet. I whooped her ass making sure I popped her ass in the mouth a few times for coming at me crazy. When Mr. Jones along with a few other guards pulled me off of her I walked away with a satisfied look on my face. My suspension was worth it now.

"Not you again, Yssa, this is your sixth fight this year." Mrs. White, the senior assistant principal shrieked.

"Everybody always fucking with me. I was minding my business when all that drama approached me." I sucked my teeth.

"You expect me to believe that in all the six times you had to sit in this chair in front of me for fighting, none of it was your fault?"

"That's exactly what I'm saying." I replied.

"When are you going to hold yourself accountable for your actions?" Mrs. White shook her head.

"When my actions are my fault. I don't fuck with anyone here,. I stay in my lane but bitches stay fucking with me like I'm a pie ass hoe or some shit." I fussed.

"Language!"

"I'm just telling it like it is."

"Yssa, you are a very bright young lady but I'm afraid that this suspension was your final straw. I have no choice but to file for expulsion."

"Do what you gotta do." I shrugged.

"This careless attitude you have will not take you far in life."

"Write up my paperwork so I can go." I waved Mrs. White off. I wasn't in the mood for one of her many pep talks. I heard them all and I didn't give a fuck; fuck her, fuck Kerri, fuck this school.

"I'm going to have to call your foster mother so she can sign off on the paperwork. I will also provide her with a list of alternative schools she can enroll you in. You may not care now but having an education is important. You are very smart Yssa. I never met someone who can miss the amount of school you did and still pass their classes. You have a lot of potential but it's up to you to apply it." She lectured while picking up the phone and dialing Katie's number. Signing my portion of the forms, I rose from the chair and sat in the lobby awaiting Katie.

When Katie arrived, if looks could kill I would be dead. She stormed past me and walked into Mrs. White's office without uttering a hello. Fifteen minutes later, Katie walked out with a folder filled with paperwork apologizing for my behavior, they said their goodbyes and we were on our way.

"Dammit Yssa! Your lil ass can't do shit right!" She vented.

"Can I have my money so I can get on about my business." I sucked my teeth.

"I don't know why I deal with your ass." She dug into her purse, pulling out the money, tossing the bills at me.

"I would whoop your ass for that disrespectful ass shit but I ain't gon waste my energy on your old ass." I huffed.

"Make sure you sign your ass up for one of these damn alternative schools." She threw the folder at me. "I swear if the social worker come to my house I'm giving ya ass up!" Katie ranted.

"Girl, I'll be eighteen soon; fuck you and them."

"You the fucking devil, I swear." Shooting me a look of disgust Katie walked off leaving me behind.

Calling a cab, I headed to Walmart and bought me a bigger bag so I could go boosting. Venturing my way through Sawgrass Mills Mall, I went from store to store and filled my bag up with shit. After hitting up Bath and Body Works, I called it a day. I had more room to grab more shit but I wasn't trying to be greedy and risk getting caught. With a bag filled with stolen goodies, I called up another cab and headed home with plans on locking up all of my stolen goodies before heading to the nail salon.

"What the fuck!" I breathed out when I spotted all of my things thrown on the lawn.

"Wait right here, don't leave." I begged the cabbie before jumping out.

"Iesha! Iesha!" I yelled banging on the door. When she didn't answer I used my foot.

"What the fuck you want?" Tony asked pushing the door open.

"Where Iesha at man?" My heart pounded wildly in my chest as I paced back and forth in attempt to calm my anger.

"What you need with my bitch?" He snarled.

"I need to know why she put all my shit out after I paid two months' rent!" I hollered.

"I don't know what you think this is but this my house. I run shit around here." Tony poked his chest out.

"Oh yeah, well I'mma need for y'all to run me back my money." I gritted.

"Nah lil mama, see that's where you got me fucked up at, I ain't giving you shit, hoe!"

"Fuck this shit, I'm calling the police." I grunted.

"Pick up that phone and I'll blast your ass before you can dial '9'." He growled producing a gun.

My words got caught in my throat as I tried my hardest to conceal the fear that radiated through my body.

"Uh huh, talk all that shit now." Tony taunted me.

Backing away from the door, I went to the lawn where my suitcases were scattered everywhere.

"No!!" I cried when I realized that the locks were popped off.

Digging in the suitcase I used to stash my money, I felt the lining for the sock that all my bills were neatly folded in. When I couldn't find it, I tossed everything out on the damp grass and began to frantically search for all the money I had left to my name.

"I got that cash up off you too; who the stupid hoe now." Tony laughed aiming his gun at me. "You got five minutes to get the fuck off my lawn before I shoot your ass for trespassing."

A feeling of defeat consumed me as I fixed my clothes back into the suitcase. Tears gathered in my eyes as I fought with myself not to let them fall. Here I was homeless and broke with the exception of the three hundred dollars I had tucked in my bra. My chest felt heavy as if someone had their heavy feet on me, pressing down, hard. I began to panic when rain started to pour from the sky. Making my way back to the cab with my bags in tow I allowed the tears that I was so desperately holding in to fall.

"Are you ok?" The cabbie asked.

"Yes, take me to Holiday Park, please." I croaked.

The cab driver offered me a look of sympathy before helping me with my suitcases. While he drove me to my destination, I stared at the window allowing my tears to flow freely. I was now back at square one, I wanted to beg Katie to allow me to come back but I knew the chances of that happening was slim to none; for one, my pride wouldn't allow me to beg and the ill feelings she harbored against me for her husband wouldn't allow her to accept me back into her home. Tonight, I had to worry about finding a location for my things. In the morning, I knew what I had to do. The stroll would be my best friend until I made enough money to make my next move.

Chapter Three

YSSA

Gathering the trash from the McDonald's I ate, I threw it in the trash. Taking a seat on the benches I watched as the fellas finished up their basketball game and decided to call it a night. It was close to ten o'clock at night and I still had no plans on what I was going to do with my things. For now, they were on the floor underneath the bleachers while I awaited everyone to clear the basketball court. My plan for now was to sneak into the bathroom before the park rangers locked up the door, that way I would at least have somewhere to lay my head for the night.

"Alright bruh I'mma get up with you later." One of the dudes called out to his friends as he walked over to where he was sitting.

I watched as he reached under the bleachers for his gym bag, his eyes fell on my suitcases before looking up at me.

"Mind your business." I snapped at him.

"You from Mr. Hart's class right, Yssa?" He asked.

Tearing my gaze away from my bags, I looked up at him and immediately realized who he was, Pierre. Pierre was an all-star around school. He ran track, played baseball, soccer, football, and basketball. His grades were exceptional hence us being in the same AP classes; he had everything; except the popularity around school.

Even though Pierre was a varsity jock, he didn't fit in with the other jocks. He was funny looking. His hair was wild and nappy, his face was oily and filled with pimples, and his mouth held a gap so wide it looked as if he was missing a tooth. The only thing he had going for him as far as looks was his body. To be seventeen, he stood at 5'9 weighing about two hundred and fifty pounds. I remember seeing his ass with his shirt off one day, drooling at how well defined and sculpted his six-pack was. Neck down Pierre looked like a Greek God; it was just the face fucking him up.

"Yeah, why? Wassup?" I chewed the inside of my cheeks.

"I ain't trying to be in your business but..."

"Then don't!" I cut him off. "Shit!" I scoffed feeling the rain starting to come down. Florida was so fucking bipolar. Hopping off the bleachers, I reached for my things.

"You need help?" He offered, reaching for my bags.

He held all of my bags only leaving the bag filled with the stolen merchandise for me to carry. Jogging towards the pavilion we stood under there for shelter for the rain. In silence, we stood there watching the rain with our thoughts.

"The park about to close in a few minutes." Pierre broke the silence.

"I know, I'm waiting for it to close."

"You need me to help you with your bags, or is someone coming to get you?" He continued his interrogating me.

"Why you all up in my business?"

"I mean, it's late as fuck and you out here in the rain with bags. I'm just being a gentlemen." He replied catching me off guard.

"Well, since you want to be a gentlemen so bad help me carry my bags to the bathroom before the park ranger comes."

"Why?" He probed.

"You nosey." I rolled my eyes. "I'm homeless alright and the minute you help me I can secure my bed for the night." I replied with no shame. I had no room for shame. I was homeless with hopes of sleeping in a dirty bathroom stall for the night.

"The bathroom so damn dirty." He frowned.

"Well, I have no choice; are you going to help me or what?"

"Yeah, let's go before the ran start up." Pierre began walking in the opposite direction.

"Stop playing man; the bathroom that way." I fussed. I was not in the mood to play.

"I know but you can crash at my crib until you figure out your arrangements."

"I don't know you like that."

"Come on, man; do I look like I'll try some crazy shit?"

"I don't know. It be the weird ones that be crazy as fuck."

"That's cold as fuck, but on the real, I just wanna help you."

"Why? You tryna get some pussy outta me?" I side-eyed him. If I had to fuck for a bed to stay in I was down but Pierre would just have to hit it from the back or something.

"Nah, my mama raised me right. It wouldn't feel right to leave you out here, all the homeless people come up here to sleep."

"I'll fit right in then." I shrugged.

"Shut up and come on before we miss the last bus to my house." He dragged me by the wrist.

"What ya mama gon say if she see me sleeping in your house?"

"My mom is a nurse; she works graveyard shift. By the time she comes home we'll be gone for school."

"Alright, but I got mace and a knife if you try something stupid."

"Alright, cool." Crossing the busy street we made it just in time to catch the bus.

Pierre paid both of our ways before carrying my things to the back of the bus. Taking a seat in the row across from him I prayed I wasn't walking into some crazy type of cult shit. Although no one bullied Pierre he was one of those high schoolers that stayed to himself; the last thing I needed was to be a pawn in some little crazy plan like shooting up the school. Pulling me from my thoughts, I watched as Pierre reached for the string, pulling on it alerting the bus driver that the next stop was the stop.

The neighborhood we entered was a nice, middle class family type of neighborhood. There was a lot of beautiful houses on the block filled with bright, beautiful colored lawns and expensive cars in the driveway. The bus came to a stop, Pierre helped me to my feet, allowing me to walk ahead of him before grabbing my bags and following me.

"Up this way." He pointed to the house that was five houses down.

"That's your house?" I questioned.

"Yeah, well my mom's house." He chuckled.

"Ya mama making bank and you riding the bus?" I joked.

"My mom's don't spoil me; she makes me work hard for everything I got. I even got a job." He shrugged.

Nodding my head, I licked my lips and followed Pierre to the beautiful light brown house that had a hint of a darker brown painted around the outer parts. The lights on the walkway lit up as we made our way to the front door. Placing my bags down, Pierre reached for his house key, granting us access to the cool dark house that smelt like Christmas cookies.

"My mom is a neat freak; she loves cleaning up and burning candles. We have wall plugs all over the place." He answered as if he was reading my mind.

"Ain't nothing wrong with being neat." I nodded my head in approval. The two story home was simply amazing. You could tell Pierre's mother spent a lot of time with her head buried in one of those home decorating magazine. Her house looked as if it could be featured on one of those covers.

"There's two bedrooms down this hallway, one belonging to me, the other for my best friend, Tommy. My mom's room and her office is upstairs. I barely go up there and she rarely comes down here; she respects my privacy as I do hers." He spoke leading me to his room.

"I know why she don't come in here; this shit is messy as fuck!" I scoffed.

"I'm a guy." He shrugged.

"A dirty one at that." I sucked my teeth. "This ain't gon work; you need to clean up." I ordered as if this was my household.

"Really?" He side-eyed me.

"Yup, unless you want me to take my ass in that pretty ass living room and cop a squat on the couch." I challenged.

"Nah, I'll clean up."

I stood by the door and watched as Pierre cleaned his huge room.

He cleared his king sized bed that was covered with clothes, sorted them out and took them down to the laundry. He then sprinkled the floor with carpet freshener before vacuuming. While he did that I decided to help out by wiping down the dust from the dressers; that was the least I could do. As I assisted him with cleaning up, I stopped and admired his room. In my seventeen years of life never have I experienced something so lavish. Across from his king sized stood a dresser that sat a huge flat panel TV. Nobody really had flat screens; you had to have money to own one of those.

In the back corner of his room was a massive walk-in closet. Next to that a shelf filled with all of his trophies and medals. Just like every teenage boy his walls was covered with posters of sports, women and Jordan shoe boxes. In the far corner was a desk equipped with an all-in-one computer and printer. A photo of him and his father hung on the wall above his desk, and just as I was going to ask where his father was my eyes landed on the obituary.

"Sorry for your loss." Was the words that escaped my lips.

"Thank you." He replied looking over at the picture. His father's death was still fresh, two years ago fresh. I felt like shit for possibly opening a can of emotions.

"This clean enough for you?" He asked.

"Yup." I smiled.

"I'll put your clothes in my closet. I'm not really into fashion so I don't have much stuff in there." He offered.

"Thank you."

"No problem; there's a bathroom through that door..." he pointed to the bathroom that was adjoined to his room, "I'm about to heat up some leftovers, you hungry?"

"Yeah." I nodded.

The cheeseburgers, small fries and coke I scarfed down barely did anything for me but I was on a budget so the dollar menu was the only thing I could splurge on at the moment.

Once Pierre was gone, I searched through my suitcase for something to wear, grabbed my shower things and headed for the bathroom. Relieved that the bathroom was cleaned, I removed my clothes and scrubbed the stress from my day away. Prolonging my shower, I stood under the hot water, enjoying the feel of the steam on my skin until the water grew cold.

"I was about to come in there and check in on you." Pierre spoke with a mouth filled with food.

The aroma from the BBQ meatloaf, mashed potatoes, mac and cheese, and cabbage forced an unrecognizable sound from my stomach.

"I was just using up all the hot water."

"Women." He shook his head. "Your food is right there." He pointed to the TV tray that was covered with a canary yellow glass plated filled with food next to a Grape Chek soda.

"This is good." I mumbled.

"Ma know how to cook. Do you know how to cook?"

"Of course." I honestly replied.

I had a thing for watching the cooking channel. I would even talk to myself while I was cooking as if I was on one of those shows.

"Why are you homeless?" Pierre asked after fifteen minutes of silence.

"Do you want the long version or the short?" I forked some meatloaf then stuffed it in my mouth.

"Well, ain't shit to do so give me the long version."

"Alright." I cleared my throat. "My mother was homeless, how ironic." I chuckled. "She fell in love with another homeless man and got pregnant with me. She couldn't take care of me so she named me, wrote this letter, placed me in a basket, and sat me in front of the church. In the letter, she basically explained to me that she was in no position to take care of me and that I was better off in the hands of someone else that could; she wrote that she named me Yssa because that name means, independence, self-confidence, positivity, filled with purpose and the ability to learn from your mistakes. She explained that she put a lot of thought into my name and if she couldn't give me anything she would make sure I had a powerful name." I took a sip of my soda.

"I got adopted really fast since I was a newborn and people loved new babies. I lived with my adoptive parents until the age of fourteen. My adoptive mom used to get abused by my adoptive father, it got so bad that he beat her until she was almost dead and then set the house on fire with the both of us still inside. When she recovered, she took him back and the abuse continued until they declared her unfit and took me away. From there, I was bounced from foster home to foster home. My last foster home I was with this lady who thought me fucking her sick ass brother for money was normal. She taught me that pussy came with a price but got mad and wanna kick me out because I fucked her husband." I chuckled. Pierre on the other hand looked at me as if he was about to pee in his pants.

"Anyways, she put me out and I met Iesha. Me and Iesha worked the same block except she had a pimp and I was just sleeping with men for money. One night, she overheard me asking one of them men to get me a hotel room since I was a minor and couldn't get one with my ID, so she stepped in and said she had a room for me to rent. I was renting from her until her pimp tried to recruit me and he basically put me out because I wasn't with it. If I was going to sell my pussy I was going to do that shit on my terms." I smacked my lips.

The look on Pierre's face was priceless. At that moment, you could hear a pin drop on the floor, that how quiet the room was. Using the silence to my advantage, I continued to eat my food not caring that Pierre was looking like he was about to have a heart attack. He asked; that's his fault for being nosey.

"Damn." He finally spoke.

"Yup."

"I could hook you up with a job at my Pop's Supermarket, my uncle own it." He offered.

"Thank you but no thank you. I need some fast money not some seven-twenty-five minimum wage job." I waved him off.

"Well, you can stay here as long as you want to."

"Until your mom catches me."

"Don't worry about that; we got school in the morning."

"I got kicked out." I sucked my teeth.

"They kicked you out for that fight you had with Kerri?"

"Yup."

"Damn, that's fucked up."

"It is." I sighed. "It's cool tho. I don't need school anyways.

"You don't?"

"Nah, I'm self-made, I get it out the mud. I may be down now but give me a few weeks. I'll be back on my feet. Good looking out Square." I cheesed, kissing him on the cheeks, the side that wasn't infected with bumps.

"Square?" He frowned.

"Yup cuz you a square ass jit, lame ass." I joked.

"Shut the fuck up Cherry." She spat at me.

"Cherry?"

"Yup, because them little ass titties look like cherries." He replied causing us to burst into a fit of laughter.

Chapter Four

PIERRE

.

"Pierre, my nigga, I'm home!" Tommy burst into my room.

Jumping out of my sleep, I looked over at Yssa who was soundly sleeping before gazing up at my best friend Tommy.

"Oh shit, my bad fam." He grinned looking over at Yssa. Her bare thighs was exposed, subconsciously I covered her with the blanket.

"Get the fuck outta here nigga. I'll come out in a few." I tossed my pillow at the door.

"Alright fam." Tommy laughed before pulling the door closed.

Getting out of the bed, I was careful not to disturb Yssa; it's been a month since she's been living with me and our bond was indescribable. At first, I was really feeling her and wanted to shoot my shot but when she friend zoned me, by referring to me as her best friend, I accepted the title and pushed all my feelings to the side. It was hard, but I learned how to separate how I really felt about her in order to salvage our friendship.

Yssa was the true definition of a diamond in the rough; she was beautiful, smart, and funny; however, she couldn't see that. She had the potential to become a great chef running a high end restaurant yet she always sold herself short. To her, if the money wasn't quick she didn't want it. I hated that she slept with men for money, that shit bothered me so much that I started breaking her off my paycheck just so she could stop that shit but Yssa was Yssa and whatever she wanted to do she did it.

After brushing my teeth and washing my face, I crept out of the room careful to not disturb Yssa, locking the door behind me. Walking down the long hallway I spotted Tommy at the kitchen table letting his boys know that he was home. Tommy and I was like night and day but we were the best of friends due to our mothers being best friends.

When Tommy's mother got arrested for murdering his father because she caught him cheating on her my mother took him in. Growing up together me and Tommy developed an unbreakable bond; he was there for me as I was for him; however, he was a menace and I was a school boy.

Tommy wanted to follow in his father's foot step and become a kingpin. Whereas I wanted to go to college, get a degree and go pro in playing basketball. Since Tommy's father was one of the biggest drug lords to hit South Florida in his time, the streets showed Tommy mad love giving him an upper hand in the game. By the age of fourteen, Tommy was on the block wreaking havoc running in and out of juvie. On Tommy's eighteenth birthday, he got caught up in some shit and ended up spending a year in jail.

"Moms told me you was getting out next month." I spoke reaching in the fridge for a protein shake.

"Them crackas let me go early." He broke down some weed. "You burning?" He asked.

"Yeah, fire it up." I gulped down my drink.

"Wassup with shorty you laid up with? That's your girl?" He quizzed.

"Nah fam; she just a homie."

"You got a homie that fine laying up in ya bed and you ain't hitting that?" His eyes narrowed in at me.

"We just cool, fam; That's my peoples." I waved him off.

"Well shit, put me down." Tommy licked his licks. A twinge of jealous pierced my heart, and I knew without a doubt if Tommy got at Yssa she would fuck with him.

Unlike me, Tommy was a ladies' man. He was a light skin brother and although he was shorter and smaller than me the females went crazy off his boyish looks and thug persona. Before he went to jail Tommy used to have different broads running in and out of his room like clockwork. I knew his kind; Tommy was a womanizer. At nineteen, he had two baby mamas that he was still fucking. Even if Yssa didn't find me attractive, I wasn't the type to hate on her if she did decide to date some other nigga as long as he wasn't Tommy.

"Nah, leave her alone; she not like that." I reached for the blunt.

"Alright fam, you got that." He chuckled. "Ma dukes met her?"

"Yeah, but she don't know she's living here." I took a long pull of the blunt.

"Shorty living here?" He quizzed.

"Yeah for a month now; she got into it with her peoples so I let her move in until shit blow over." I lied even though Tommy was my dawg. I respected Yssa enough not to go into details about personal information she confided in me about.

"How you pull that shit off? Ma Dukes used to stay busting in on me and my hoes."

"For one, we not in there fucking all loud and shit but she be chilling around the house with me but instead of going home she just sneak back to my room when my mom either go to work or to bed."

"Smart ass nigga. You need to be hitting that shit tho, that ass fat."

"Nah, she just the hommie." I assured him.

"Alright." He shrugged his shoulders.

"Pierre, you'll walk with me to the store." Yssa walked out of the room dressed in a pair of tight shorts that her ass hung out of, one of my white tank tops that she tied into a knot underneath her breasts with a pair of white thong flip flops on her feet. Her hair was wild and curly, and although she hated it that way I loved how the hint of gold in her curls matched her bright skin to perfection. Yssa was the epitome of beautiful, there was no denying that.

Since my mom was at a nurse's convention in New York for the week, Yssa was free to roam around as she pleased.

"Hey best friend." Tommy joked licking his lips.

"Wassup." She waved at Tommy. "Square, go get ready so we could go." She playfully punched me in the chest."

Looking from her to Tommy, I contemplated if I wanted to leave them alone together.

"You coming or not?" Yssa impatiently asked.

"Yeah, let me get dressed." I took another toke of the blunt and passed it back to Tommy.

Rushing back to my room, I quickly got dressed and made it to the front door within minutes.

"I'll get up with you later." I dabbed Tommy up before walking out the door.

"I see your best friend is home. Does that mean you're going to start ditching me cuz um I don't fuck with nobody; you my only friend." Yssa smacked her lips.

"Nah, I wouldn't do you like that." I assured her. "What you getting out the store?"

"Some pads and shit." She spoke as we headed to my uncle shop.

Engaging in small conversation, we walked to the store. Holding the door open for her, I allowed her to walk in first before I followed closely. Unintentionally, my eyes fell on her ass, staring at her apple bottom, admiring the way her booty cheeks played peek-a-boo with every step she took. I allowed my eyes to wonder for a few minutes before tearing my gaze away from her back side.

"What's good son?" My uncle greeted me. "You here to pick-up your check?" He asked.

"Oh snap, I forgot today was pay day. I came here with Yssa; she needed to grab a few personal items." I looked over at Yssa as she searched the shelves for her feminine products.

"Wassup with the two of you?" He asked. I was getting sick and tired of this question. If I had to explain that Yssa just my friend to someone else I was going to lose it.

"We just friends unc."

"Friends huh?" He chuckled.

"Yup." I firmly replied.

"Alright, let me go back here and get your check." He coughed a few times before walking towards the back.

"Unc, you need to do something about that cough." I spoke the moment he returned.

"It's just a lil cold son, nothing some lemon and honey can't fix." He replied handing me and envelope.

"Thanks man. Put her things on my tab, you can take it out of my next check."

"And you say she just a friend." My unc chuckled before ringing Yssa things up.

I could have paid for my own stuff." She fussed the moment we walked out of the store.

"I know, but I gotchu." I winked.

"Let's walk to the Check Cashing Store so I can cash my check then I'll take your fat ass to the mall to get some Chinese food.

"Mmm, mall food. You love spoiling me." She joked.

"I'm just trying to show you how a man is supposed to treat you whenever you decide to start dating." I laughed, meaning every word.

"Speaking of dating when are you going to stop playing and get with lil mama, your senior prom is coming up."

"I got my eye on a girl but she ain't checking for me like that." I smirked.

"Shame on her then because any girl alive would be lucky to have a boy like you." She stated.

Looking at her, I wondered if she meant that shit. I wondered if that was a hint she was dropping for me to ask her out. I build up the courage to do it but I couldn't get the words to leave my lips.

"Square, you good?" She asked.

"Yeah Cherry, I'm straight." I replied, lowering my head to the ground.

As much as I wanted to ask Yssa out the fear of rejection wouldn't allow me to.

Chapter Five

YSSA

"It's smelling good in here." Tommy blew out a cloud of smoke from his lips before walking over to me.

Standing directly behind me, Tommy trapped my body against his as he placed his hands on the edge of the counter cornering me in. I could smell the weed mixed with his cologne from his skin. Not only did this motherfucker look good but he smelled good too. Tommy was the type of nigga that ya mama would warn you about but since I didn't have one, I stood there enjoying his front pressed against my backside.

"What you cooking?" He asked.

"Chicken parmesan over a bed of garlic butter noodles with a side of fresh baked garlic bread." I beamed proudly. Cooking was my thing; I knew the ins and outs of the kitchen. Stepping outside of the typical box, I cooked more gourmet meals. Pierre enjoyed eating my food just as much as I enjoyed preparing it for him.

"You baked bread from scratch?" Tommy questioned.

"Yup!"

"Wow, most bitches bake the frozen shit that come out of the box."

"Well I'm not most bitches." I smacked my lips.

"No offense, just saying." He hoisted his hand in the air as if he was surrendering.

Turning to grab a plate for the food, I was able to get a good look at Tommy. His face was smooth and blemish free, complexion bright, a shade lighter than mine. His pink juicy lips were plump, his grill covered in golds, and his hair was swimming with waves deep enough to drown you if you got close enough. He was shorter than Pierre, standing about 5'7 and a lot smaller weighing one-hundred and ninety-five pounds, nonetheless he was a lot more sexier. Tommy had this pretty boy look but his eyes told a different story. The darkness in his eyes pleaded with me to turn on my heels and walk away; the danger in them screamed he was nothing but trouble but that didn't stop me for being curious.

Picking through Pierre's mom, Mary, dishes, I chose a ruby red ceramic dish to plate Pierre's food in. Setting the dish on the table, I garnished it with parsley then placed two slices of fresh bread next to it. Just as I was walking to the oven to check on my chocolate chip and peanut butter brownies Pierre was walking through the door.

"What's good bruh?" Pierre dapped Tommy up before reaching in and giving me a hug.

"Eww, you sweaty." I shooed him away.

"You know you like this sweat." He rubbed his drenched tank top on me before mushing the side of my head. "It's smelling good in here Cherry." He called out, eyes hungrily roaming over the plate of food.

"I made your plate." I handed it to him.

"Thank Cherry." He bumped me before walking to the room with his plate in his hand.

"You're welcome Square." I called out.

"Wassup with you and my hommie?" Tommy asked.

"Nothing, shit. Just like you his best friend, he's mine." I shrugged.

"Alright cool. You gon fix me a plate?" Tommy licked his lips.

"Nah. You got hands." I winked before juggling two bottles of water and my food in my hand while making my way to Pierre's room.

"Cherry, this shit is good." Pierre spoke in between bites.

"I did my thang, didn't I." I blushed.

"Yes ma'am. You should really start taking this more seriously." He urged.

"I hear you." I rolled my eyes.

"Nah for real C, you could make some good money, open you a lil spot, and you'll be set." He continued.

"I'm a high school dropout; how you expect me to do all of that. I'm about to be eighteen, you're about to graduate, the only thing that's on my mind is stacking my bread so I could be straight."

"You can always get your GED. Matter fact..." He got up from the bed. "I got you a GED book with the practice test, not that you need it, but it came with the registration packet." He handed everything to me.

"Registration packet?" I questioned looking from him to the books.

"Yes. I registered you in the GED class. All you have to do is go in and take the test whenever you're ready."

"Why would you do that shit without my permission?" I snapped.

"What you getting mad for?"

"I'm getting mad because you're all in my fucking business trying to make decision about my life for me."

"C, I ain't mean nothing by it." Pierre looked at me with sad eyes. "I just want to push you to your fullest potential. I want so much for you because you deserve it." He lowered his head.

"I know Square, but you gotta let me figure this shit out on my own. Don't force it on me, alright?"

"Ok cool. You got weed? Man fucking with you I'mma need a blunt." Pierre sucked his teeth.

"Go wash your stank ass and I'll roll up.

While Pierre Took his shower, I reached into the slit that tore into one of my suitcases and retrieved the sock that held my new stash. With the money I was making from sleeping with dudes and by selling stolen merchandise I had about forty-five hundred dollars saved. Time wasn't on my side, I needed about ten G's saved up so I could apply for a low income apartment. Placing my money back, I sealed the slit closed and reached for the bag of weed so I could roll up. By the time Pierre got out of the shower I had three blunts rolled and ready.

"Why don't you do something with your hair?" I asked when he walked into the room with that nappy ass fro.

"If you not gonna braid it, shut up!" Pierre plopped down on the ground reaching for a blunt. Placing the tip in his mouth he fired it up and inhaled a deep pull.

"Come sit right here so I can braid it for you." I sucked my teeth.

"Yo, you for real? You know how to braid?" He asked me.

"Yeah, I can do a lil something, something; now hurry up before I change my mind.

Gathering all of my hair supplies, I motioned for Pierre to sit between my legs so I could braid his hair. Passing the blunt back and forth, we talked, laughed and jammed to the radio while I braided his hair in simple braids going back. Growing up, I never had friends or knew what it felt like to have a person genuinely love you for you and not because they were expecting something in return.

Meeting Pierre was the best thing that happened to me. Not because he gave me a place to stay when I was homeless but because he believed in me when I didn't believe in myself. He was able to see past my damages, creating a beautiful image of me. I loved seeing myself through his eyes; the way he spoke so much purpose in my life, breathing hope into the way he is so selfless with me. Pierre had become my protector, my perception of how a man should be; he was so pure and I was tainted. We were so different yet in sync with one another.

"I'mma give you a makeover!" I announced finishing up my last braid.

"For what?" Pierre sucked his teeth.

"Nigga, shut the fuck up and get dressed so we can go." I smacked him on the back of the head and swung my legs around so I could stand up.

"I ain't really tryna spend money on unnecessary shit." He sighed.

"You got all these fly ass kicks, but no clothes to match. If I watch you put on another black tee with a pair of Dickies, I'mma scream!"

"Man." He gripped his bottom lip with his teeth.

There wasn't much I could do about his looks so I figured I could at least fix up his appearance.

"Hurry up and come on!" Standing in front of Pierre's walk-in closet, I removed my clothes, while searching for something else to wear.

With Pierre, I've developed a level of comfortability. I was able to walk-around in my bra and panties, fart around him, take a shit while he showered, just be me without the fear of being judged. Once we were dressed, I grabbed my oversized purse and tossed it over my shoulders.

"Oh, hell nah!" Pierre waved me off once he realized I had my shoplifting purse on.

"Shut up, Square and let's go." I snapped.

"Cherry, if your ass get caught, I'm leaving you." He sucked his teeth.

"No you won't." I stuck my tongue out at him before walking out of the room bumping into Tommy who was walking some broad to the door. Deceiving me, my eyes traveled down to his bare chest landing on his dick print.

Damn! I licked my lips.

"Y'all out?" Tommy asked sizing me up before turning to Pierre.

"Yeah, I'll get up with you later." Dapping Tommy up, the boys said their goodbyes and we were on our way.

The entire bus ride to the mall, my mind stayed on Tommy. Pierre expressed how he wasn't good enough for me, forbade me to deal with him, but the rebel in me couldn't resist. Arriving at the shopping center, we made our way to Marshalls first. I already knew what size Pierre was, so I didn't really need him to do shit but be my lookout. While I browsed the men's clothing, I picked out different outfits to match the shoes he had in his closet. With Pierre standing over me, I was able to pop the tags, slip them in my bags and move on to the next rack.

Once the bag was stuffed, we walked out of the store undetected. I was a pro at what I did. I learned every store I boosted out of before I got to work. I studied who the employees were, the managers, and the security guards making a mental not of which shift they worked.

Leaving the mall, we headed to the barbershop so Pierre could get a fresh line-up. The braids were sick, and I knew without a doubt he was going to walk through those halls killing shit once I got done with him. Our last stop was Family Dollar where I purchased some acne wash for him. I wasn't sure what was going to work so I bought a couple of them.

"You didn't have to do all of this." Pierre spoke as we walked back to his house.

"You didn't have to let me, a stranger, move into ya spot but you did." I licked my lips.

"It's all love, Cherry." He wrapped his arm around my neck.

"I know Square. I love you, too." I beamed leaning my head into his arms.

Chapter Six

YSSA

"What the fuck?" I groaned wiping the sleep from my eyes. Sitting up in the hotel bed, I searched the room for Alex, but he was nowhere in sight. Looking over at the nightstand, my eyes scanned the old chipped table top for my cash but it wasn't there.

"This fuck nigga man." I huffed kicking the blankets from my body."

When I realized my panties were gone, I knew what was up. My eyes traveled to the empty cup of Hennessey that sat by the hotel's phone, and it was then I realized this nigga must have slipped me something that made me drowsy. I was never the type of trick to fall asleep in bed with one of my John's unless he was paying me to. Alex wanted a quick fuck, one that cost him two-hundred dollars. Rage filled my body thinking how this fool had to get one over on me. All he had to do was handle his business and give me my money, but the fact that he tried to get one over on me further enraged me.

Stomping to the bathroom, I quickly gave myself a hoe bath slipping my dress over my head. Picking up my panties, I stuffed them in my bag, reached for my flip-flops and rushed out of the room making my way to the block. Alex was a middle level dope boy. He wasn't getting fee like some of the niggas on the block but he wasn't hurting either. I met him through his homie Rallo, a dude I dealt with on and off. Rallo loved sliding between my thighs but he had problem affording me. He was one of those John's who would call on the first of the month when he received his disability check.

The minute I stepped on 13th street I spotted Alex, Rallo, and Tommy chopping it up. Any other time, I would have walked the other way, avoiding Tommy and the temptation he brought but today I was on a mission. I needed my money and I was going to get it. Every little bit counted.

"You got something for me?" I walked up on Alex.

"Man." He licked his lips. "Get from around here!" Alex waved me off.

"Nah, give me my money!" I snapped.

I didn't care that he was trying to play me in front of his friends. I would act a fool if I had to embarrass myself if need be.

"What's good Yssa, you straight?" Tommy butted in.

"This hoe on some other shit, Tommy, fuck her." Alex snarled.

"Fuck me?" I chuckled. "What type of nigga put a roofie in a female's drink so he could get some pussy without paying for it. You came to me seeking my service, now you need to pay up nigga! Matter fact, your tab just jumped up to five hundred dollars for raping me!" I screamed.

"Aye, shut the fuck up with all of that rah- rah shit." Alex grabbed me by my throat.

WHAMP!

Tommy punched Alex in the face forcing him to let me go as he stumbled to the ground.

"You raping females, my niggas?" Tommy fumed.

"The bitch wanted two hundred dollars to fuck so I fucked." Alex cried.

"Did you pay her?"

"Nah, she was sleep fam."

"Because you drugged me!!!" I yelled.

"Chill out ma." Tommy looked over at me before turning his attention back to Alex.

"Give the shorty her money."

"All five hundred of them dollars!" I smacked my lips.

"Five hundred? Bitch you sleep." Alex reached in his pocket, peeled off two hundred dollars bills from a knot then tossed it at me.

WHAMP! WHAMP!

Tommy hit him with a two-piece, splitting his lip in the process.

"Come on, man." Alex winced in pain as blood gushed from the gash on his mouth.

Give her everything that's in your pocket." Tommy ordered.

"Are you for real?"

"I'm dead ass. If you want to keep working this block do what the fuck I say or get dealt with!" Tommy ordered.

The way he dealt with Alex was a turn-on for me. I enjoyed watching him belittle that motherfucker. My eyes twinkled as I watched Tommy strip Alex of all his money before handing the knot to me.

"It ain't a good look, raping females and shit. I should whoop your ass for that shit." Tommy growled.

"My bad fam."

"Nah, apologize to her." Tommy pointed in my direction.

At this point, I didn't give a fuck about what Alex had to say. He taught me a valuable lesson; from now own, payment was due before I spread my legs open. An apology wasn't going to fix shit. I was already a fucking mess. Too far gone, and I couldn't be fixed.

"My bad ma." Alex apologized.

"Boy fuck you." I sucked. "Thank you, Tommy." I smiled at him before walking off.

"Ay shorty, wait up." Tommy called out jogging over to me.

"Wassup?" I licked my lips.

If being sexy was against the law, then Tommy would have been in jail. It was close to ninety degrees outside so his only attire was a white pair of baller shorts that hung loosely around his waist displaying the band of his boxers. A fresh, out the box pair of all-white Air Force ones adorned his feet. The fitted cap that he pulled over his head did little to block the sunrays from bouncing all over his face. His chest was bare giving me a clear view of his tatted up stomach.

"Why you sell pussy?" He asked.

"Why you sell drugs." I rebutted.

"I feel you." He chuckled. "But damn, don't fuck with Alex square ass no mo."

"I know. Why Alex pussy up like that when you came from him? You his boss or something?" I questioned.

"Something like that." He shrugged.

"If someone was looking to purchase some pussy how would he go about doing it? I mean, do he get to take a whiff of the pussy? Sample it or some shit?" Tommy asked with a chuckle.

"Nah, he pay me my money and get what he get." I sucked my teeth.

"How much?"

"Five hundred." I tossed at him fucking with him.

"Oh alright." He sized me up. His gaze then ventured off to the other side of the street where a white car pulled up.

"Be easy out here ma, I'm out. Go put that money up before you get back out here on these streets."

"I know how to hustle." I waved him off.

"Alright Ms. Trap Star." Tommy hiked up his gym shorts before walking off to the impatient driver who was now honking the horn.

I lingered around a bit to get a glimpse of the driver. When the car did a wide U-Turn in the middle of the road, I was able to look inside. My eyes landed on the woman then to the backseat where a little boy was fastened.

"That must be his baby mama." I spoke to myself as I made my way to the house.

Chapter Seven

PIERRE

"Hey, Pierre you taking anyone to the prom?" Crystal asked hoisting the books she was carrying on her hips.

Since she was struggling with her books, I grabbed them out of her hand and walked with her.

"Thank you." She blushed. "Back to my question; you have a date?"

"Yes, I'm going with my best friend." I replied. "Why, wassup?"

"I just wanted to see if you wanted to go with me, that's all." She shrugged.

"I already promised her she could come with me since she didn't get to go to her prom." I licked my lips. "Put your number in my phone and we can arrange me taking you out." I flirted.

"I'd like that." She beamed reaching for my phone.

Girls that never really paid me any attention started to approach me since Yssa switched up my dress code and started braiding my hair in different styles every week. That and me being a varsity jock boosted up my popularity.

"Make sure you call me." Crystal smiled.

Crystal had the prettiest brown skin I'd ever seen. She was slim but built with a nice ass and toned legs due to her running track. She was one of the fastest with a full ride scholarship to college because of it.

Crystal was a sweet girl that made good grades; she didn't get in trouble, and she was still one of the few girls in high school that still clung on to her virginity. All in all, Crystal was the right girl, the kind my mother would be proud to claim as her daughter-in-law.

"I'll get up with you later." Walking her to her car, then I opened the door, waited for her to get in before handing her the books.

"You need a ride?" She questioned.

"Nah, my best friend waiting on me." I poked my head in the driver's side window.

Although Crystal was driving a 2002 Toyota Camry, the inside of her car was clean and smelt like sunflowers.

"Call me later?" She stuck the key in the ignition.

"Yup." I smiled, stepping away from the car so she could pull off.

"I see you bestie." Yssa cooed walking up on me.

"Just chill." I waved her off as we began our walk.

I had work tonight and she would usually just sit around at the supermarket with me until she dipped off and handled her business. The more I stressed her about having sex with men for money, the further I pushed her away. One day, I got on her ass about it and she got so mad that she left my house and didn't come back until three days later. I was at the point where I just accepted her for who she was the same way I accepted Tommy and his occupation.

"I see you macking down on the ladies; do tell." She probed.

"That's just Crystal."

"Her square ass." She chuckled. "That's a good look, tho; she's a good girl."

"I know. Wassup with you? What you did today?" I changed the subject.

"Shit. I'mma start looking for some apartments, tho. I saved up enough, plus my birthday is around the corner." She huffed.

"I hear you." I replied keeping my thoughts to myself.

"Speak your mind, Square."

"I'm straight Cherry."

"Mmhmm." She hummed as we made our way to Popeye's to grab something to eat.

Yssa paid for the food, and I purchased the weed. Before it was time for me to clock in, we sat at the park smoking, eating and talking.

"I passed my GED test." Yssa spoke while smacking on some chicken.

"Yo, you for real?" I questioned.

"Yup!"

"Damn, congrats ma!" I pulled her in for a hug. "And your nappy headed ass was so pissed when I brought it up."

"I told you I had to do it on my own time." She rolled her eyes.

"What's next?"

"What you mean?"

"You give any thoughts of going to college?" I asked.

"With what money? I'm slanging pussy to survive. I don't have enough twat to sell to be able to afford school." She shrieked.

"There's scholarships and shit." I blew out a cloud of smoke.

"Square, chill alright. I'm good. Now, let's go before you're late for work."

While I stocked groceries, Yssa sat on a bench texting on her phone. When my shift was over, we headed to the house. Since my mother didn't leave anything prepared for dinner, Yssa decided to whip up some baked chicken, green beans and white rice. Tommy joined us for dinner, we smoked, watched movies then I retired to my room to hit up Crystal.

"Shit!" I groaned stretching my limbs. Glancing over at the time, I realized it was four in the morning.

I was caked up on the phone with Crystal for hours, chopping it up. She was a cool girl. Looking over to my right, I noticed Yssa wasn't beside me; she wasn't in the bathroom either so I headed to the kitchen thinking she was in there baking sweets, a hobby she enjoyed on the nights my mother was away at work.

"Where the fuck this girl at?" I spoke to myself walking through the house.

"This nigga." I chuckled as I passed by Tommy room; the door was slightly opened and moans could be heard.

"Damn daddy." A chick moaned catching me off guard. The voice was familiar... too familiar.

Turning back, I pushed the door open only to see my Yssa riding the fuck out of Tommy. I warned them woo about this relationship. I told Yssa that Tommy wasn't shit and I made it clear to Tommy that Yssa wasn't that type of chick. To watch them betray me in the worse way caused my body to fill with rage.

"This how it is?" I barked.

"Oh shit!" Yssa squeaked, grabbing the blankets to cover up her naked body.

"P, man it ain't even like that." Tommy dragged his hand over his face.

"This some fuck shit." I fumed, charging towards them.

Pushing Yssa off the bed, I reached over for Tommy and yoked his ass up crashing my fist into his jaw.

"Pierre stop!" Yssa screamed.

The fact that she was yelling for this nigga's defense sent me into overdrive. Every emotion I was feeling, I took it out on Tommy. In the past, he was known to fuck with females I had a crush on but out of all those other broads this one was different. Yssa meant something to me. I loved her... appreciated our friendship, cherished what we had but that shit wasn't enough. Tommy had to disrespect me by crossing the only line I drew.

"Pussy nigga you think you tough and shit catching me off guard." Tommy huffed.

Reaching for his gym shorts, he covered his dick before throwing his set up. Walking around Yssa who stood there yelling for us to stop, I put my hands up and prepared to fight my best friend. In the middle of his room, we went blow for blow destroying everything in the process. Punching Tommy hard in the face, I hoisted his body high in the air, slamming him down on the dresser causing the mirror to fall over and break.

"That's enough." Yssa cried, jumping in the middle of us. I had Tommy pinned down, ready to punch his lights out but the look in Yssa's face stopped me. Even though I was mad at her, she still held the ability to pull my strings. Pulling away from Tommy, I backed out of the room.

"Fuck y'all!" I huffed.

Quickly throwing on some clothes, I reached for my phone and stormed out of the house. I wasn't sure if she was awake but Crystal was the first person I dialed.

ॐ

"I never really did this before." Crystal looked up at me with so much innocence.

"We don't have to do it." I laid in the bed next to her.

Crystal came from a broken family. She didn't know who her father was and her mother was delirious, running free as if she was a careless teenager. At home, Crystal was the mother to her three siblings. She took care of them as if she birthed them. Since the incident happened a week ago, I've been staying with Crystal. Since my mother was working longer shifts in preparation for sending me off to college, she wasn't home to notice my absence. I needed to get away, and Crystal's house became my duck off spot.

"I want to do it." She turned, facing me.

I wasn't pressuring her for sex; she was pushing the issue. I've had sex before; she was the virgin. I wasn't sure what we was calling what we were doing; therefore, I wanted her to be sure she wanted to share something she would never be able to get back.

"Crystal." I groaned, as she mounted me. My dick sprang to life, begging to be freed.

"Be gentle." She kissed me on the lips.

I took my time and explored her body from head to toe. At a young age, I was pretty good at sex.

For my fifteenth birthday, Tommy was mad that I was still a virgin so he talked one of his flings into sleeping with me. At first, she wasn't with it. She was only doing it to please Tommy but when she realized I was a fast learner with a nice sized dick we continued fucking around. Since she was more experienced than I was, she taught me a lot of stuff. We would watch porn while mimicking everything that was being done. In public, she acted as if she didn't know me but behind closed doors, I was her little freak. When I contracted Trichomoniasis from her, our good time came to an end.

After getting treated, I blocked her number and never looked her way again.

"That feels so good." Crystal moaned as I explored between her thighs with my tongue. I took my time with each tongue stroke, making her feel good.

"Oh God." She quivered as her legs began to shake.

I continued to suck on her clit until her body went limp.

"I don't have a condom." I huffed.

"My mother has some, hold on." Slipping into her robe, she ran out of the room in search of the condom.

Pulling my dick out the slit of my boxers, a proud smile graced my face. I may not have been many women's first choice but my dick was big and that was all that mattered. My mother made sure I got circumcised as a baby, something I thanked her for. In class I would hear girls talking about how they hated topping off niggas with pull-backs, I wanted to pull my dick out and show them what I was carrying between my legs but I was shy as fuck when it came to females. Running my hand over my mushroom tip, I wiggled my dick from side to side awaiting Crystal's return.

"I got a Magnum." She waved the gold package in the air.

"The perfect size." I licked my lips.

"Wow." Her eyes widened as she looked down at my dick.

Reaching for the condom, I tore it open and slid it down my dick.

"You sure you wanna do this?" I asked, pulling her down on the bed next to me.

"Yes."

"No pressure."

"I wanna do this with you." She assured me.

"Alright, bet." I licked my lips before placing it against her.

My lips then traveled to her ears, neck, and breasts. She squirmed underneath me as I suckled on her right breast while using my forefinger and thumb to toy with the left one. Using my knees I pushed her legs wide apart before penetrating her. I held her waist down as I pushed myself in deep until the barrier that kept her pure tore.

"Ahhhhhhhh!!!" She cried out, tears trickling down her face.

"Sorry baby." I kissed away her tears as I slow pumped her.

Crystal's pussy felt so much better than the overused pussy I used to lose my virginity to. Her cried were soft, but the grip she held around my neck expressed that she didn't want me to stop. The ringing of my phone caught my attention. When I looked over the name *Cherry* appeared on the screen. Shaking my head, I went back to giving Crystal all of my attention.

"You wanna go to the prom with me?" I asked as I picked up the pace.

"I thought you was going with your best friend?" She breathed out.

"I was but now I wanna go with you."

"I'd like that." She smiled.

"Me too." I dipped my head down to her lips, kissing her until I felt my blood rush through my veins. Tightening my grip around her waist, I filled the condom before falling down next to her, struggling to catch my breath.

Chapter Eight

YSSA

It's been three months since I moved out of Pierre's house and into my own low-income apartment. I was hurt when he rejected my invitation to prom, inviting Crystal instead. Although I was happy for my friend, I was looking forward to sharing that day with him. Our relationship was a lot better now that we were able to sit down and talk things out. Space is what we needed from each other; once everything blew over, we were back to being best friends. Now that he was dating Crystal, he was ok with me seeing Tommy. I could tell that gesture bothered him but he gave me his blessings.

"Baby, you seen my shoes?" Tommy asked walking up on me, kissing me on the lips.

"They in the walk-in closet in the hallway." I called out.

With the help of Tommy, I was able to move into a nice two bedroom-two bathroom apartment. He paid all the bills, while I took care of the little things around the house. I was no longer sleeping with men for money, but I still held onto my boosting job.

"I'm about to pick up TJ." He spoke as he slipped his feet into his shoes.

"Alright." I sighed at the mention of him picking up his son.

I had no problem with his kids but it was the mothers that drove me crazy. Tori, TJ's mother, felt like she was entitled to Tommy because she gave him his first child, his "Jr". Even though our relationship was still new, she didn't respect it. Nesha, the mother of Tommy's daughter, Crissianna, gave less problems than Tori did. Everything with her was a fight; we hadn't come to blows yet but I was sure it was going to happen sooner or later.

"In and out." He promised, kissing me again.

While Tommy stepped out to handle his business, I continued the task of cooking and cleaning. For the first time in a long time I felt secured. I was eighteen, living in my own spot, with close to eleven thousand dollars in my bank account, an account Pierre helped me open up. Thinking of my friend, I grabbed my phone to call him but he didn't answer. With his graduation being a month away, he was working doubles trying to earn enough money to handle all of his college essentials. I thought it was cute that he put in the effort to work in attempt to ease some of the work load off his mother.

An hour later, the house was cleaned and dinner was cooked. Taking a seat on the couch, I decided to busy myself by painting my toes. After switching through three different colors, I decided to go with the mint green polish. Once my toes were dried, I walked around the house with my phone in my hand calling Tommy only to get his voicemail.

The sky grew dark, the street lights came home and there were still no signs of Tommy. Panic began to consume me as I thought the worse. Reaching for my phone, I called him again but was surprised when a female answered the phone.

"Hello." She sung into the phone.

"Where is Tommy?" I smacked my lips.

"Who? My baby daddy Tommy?" Tori chuckled.

"Nah, my man Tommy!" I spat.

"Oh, girl bye, he ain't coming home tonight; that nigga is sleep. I might think about sending him to you in the morning; it depends tho." She laughed before hanging the phone up in my face.

Rage surged through my body as I quickly got dressed in a pair of sweats, Timberlands, and a tank top. Locking up the apartment, I took the streets like a storm walking each block. I felt like a fool walking with no destination. I had no clue where Tori lived so looking for Tommy was pointless. Instead of heading back home, I called a cab and ended up in front of Pierre's house. Paying the cabbie, I got out of the car and dialed his number.

"Hello?" He answered sounding as if I had woken him out of his sleep.

"You was sleeping?" I asked.

"Nah, wassup Cherry?" He asked causing me to smile.

"Nothing Square, open the door for me. I'm outside."

"Alright." He breathed before hanging up.

Pierre came to the door shirtless, wearing nothing but a pair of NBA shorts.

"Put some damn clothes on." I playfully punched his firm chest.

"Stop hating, I'm sexy as fuck." He waved me off, leading me to his bedroom. "Why you out this late?" He locked his room door.

"I don't know." I shrugged, plopping down on his bed.

"Tommy with that fuck shit huh?" He shook his head.

"He said he was going to pick his son up. Hours later, I called his phone, and his baby mama answer the phone saying 'oh, he ain't coming home for the night' and she might think about letting him come home the next morning." I sucked my teeth.

"Ayo, Tommy is my boy and all but you don't deserve this shit." He lectured.

"Not today." I groaned.

"Nah, you need to hear this shit." Pierre snapped getting up from the bed. 'Look at yourself!" He demanded handing me a mirror.

"You are beautiful, fucking gorgeous. You are smart as fuck too. You barely looked at those GED books I bought you but you went to take the test and passed with a perfect score! You have so much potential, you are amazing, talented, everything that a good man would appreciate. As much as you want to think you and Tommy are the same, you're not! You did what you have to do in order to survive, Tommy chose his lifestyle. My mother worked hard for the both of us, Tommy always had a roof over his head, the newest gadgets and latest clothes, my mother made sure of it. All she asked is that we do well in school and worked hard. He wanted to run the streets. You had no option but to play the hand life dealt you. Stop selling yourself short ma." Pierre stood over me, forcing me to look at myself in the mirror while he talked.

Tears gathered in my eyes; I tried to hold them but I couldn't. Pierre was the only one that understood me, saw the real me. I didn't want to sleep with all those different men for money; I had to. Even though I was broken, damaged, contaminated, Pierre had the ability to see through it all. In reality, I was afraid. I was eighteen and although at the moment I was content because in the moment I had things figured out, I was nervous that time would shift and I would be back out on the streets. Which was why I depended so much on my relationship with Tommy; he offered stability.

After graduation, Pierre would be leaving for Duke University on a full paid scholarship to play basketball. His stars were aligned, and he had a plan B; the only thing I had was a nigga who was just as fucked up as I was. It wasn't the best situation but I had no choice but to except it. The sob that escaped my lips alerted Pierre, so he wrapped his arms around me and held me tightly. The scent from the bar of soap he showered with mixed with the faint smell of weed that still lingered around filled my nostrils. Pierre always smelt nice, and being in his arms always felt like home.

"Let me help you." He pleaded. Pierre was perfect, too perfect for me. I didn't deserve his friendship yet he was still here.

"I'm just so broken Pierre. I'm tired of being this broken." I blabbered, my face was wet with tears that mixed in with snot creating a mess all over my face.

"Let me fix you." He whispered, pulling his towel from the back of his chair. He used it to dry my face.

Pierre bent down and removed my shoes from my feet. He then pulled off my sweats, before removing my top. Sitting there in my bra and panties I felt ashamed for the first time. I felt unworthy of being in his presence. I wasn't good enough.

"You are perfect." He whispered as if he was connected to my thoughts.

Soon after those words left his lips, my panties fell to the ground next to my bra. Pierre pushed me back on the bed, placing his head between my legs. My legs shook, as he dipped his tongue in my center twirling it around. Unlike my previous sex partners, he was gentle. He took his time eating, sucking, and licking the orgasm out of me before standing to his feet. When Pierre dropped his pants, I wasn't surprised. I knew he was hung. With length and width, Pierre had enough dick to put any grown man to shame.

Our lips connected as we shared a passionate kiss. Spreading my legs, I gave Pierre access. I allowed him to make love to me. Thrust for thrust, I lifted my hips into him matching his every stroke. Tears trickled down my face as I felt things I shouldn't have been feeling for my best friend. My heart opened up, my stomach clenched, my mind was in a furry as my soul lifted from my body. The orgasm I experienced was too much to bare that a low growl escaped my lips before my body went limp.

"I love you Cherry." He whispered in my ear while playing in my hair.

"I love you, too, Square."

I was in bliss laying in his arms. Sex with Pierre was beautiful, magical, and it felt real. For the first time in my life, I enjoyed sex without feeling as if it was a job. Even when I had sex with Tommy, I knew I had to fuck and suck him the best in order to secure my comfortability.

"Come with me." He spoke after five minutes of silence.

"Come with you where?"

"To Duke. I can put off starting in Summer. I'll enroll for Fall classes; that way it gives us time to come up with a solid plan."

"I can't." I replied.

"Why not?" He questioned.

Looking over at my ringing phone, Tommy's name flashed across the screen. Just that quick my fairytale world was shattered as reality set in.

"I'm pregnant."

Chapter Nine

PIERRE

Eight years later...

Dressed down in a tailor-made three-piece Armani suit with a pair of red bottom loafers on my feet I stepped in G5, looking fresh to death. The two diamond studs I wore in each ear matched the diamond chain that hung from my neck and the iced out Patek that sat lovely on my wrist. I had just signed a four year one hundred and forty-five million dollar contract to play basketball in Miami and a nigga was feeling good as fuck.

"Jump Man, P!" one of my teammates called out as he waved me over to him.

"Wassup baby!" I dapped him up. Security allowed me entrance into the VIP section before blocking it off with a rope and standing guard.

"How it feels to be in Miami kid?" Duce, the three-time MVP player asked. According to Sports Center me being traded to Miami to play alongside Duce was history in the making. Together we were going to create magic.

"I'm from here, well Fort Lauderdale but it does feel good to be back home." I gulped down a shot of Hennessey.

It's been eight years since I've been in Florida. After leaving to attend Duke University eight years ago, my mother accepted a high paying General Nurse Practitioner job in Atlanta, where she married a doctor. Once I completed school and received a degree in Finance, I entered the NBA draft signing my first professional ball playing contract with Chicago. Four years and two championship rings later I was declared one of the greatest ball players of all time. When I became a free agent every team was on my trail; however, when Miami offered me the highest contract I decided to play with them.

"That's right! But check me out, I got some fye ass strippers coming to the section." He beamed with excitement.

I wasn't pressed by these strippers, Most shit that excited these ball players did nothing for me. I had my fair share of women, so I was cooling it now. Being in the blogs for being promiscuous wasn't my M.O.

"Oh shit, there they go now! It's this bad ass red bone by the name of Cherry; her ass bad as fuck."

I was uninterested in what Duce was saying until he mentioned Cherry. Looking up, my eyes met hers, and for a minute time stopped as I studied *Cherry*. Duce didn't lie when he described Yssa as being fine as fuck. Time did her body well. The thin girl I once loved was replaced with a thick, video vixen, looking chick. Her body was voluminous all over. Her breasts were now double D's, and she now possessed sharp wide hips, her stomach was still flat, her legs were never ending and her ass was fat as hell. The only thing that stayed the same was her pretty face that looked as if she hadn't aged.

"You want a dance?" She asked Duce, tearing her eyes away from mine.

"I'll take one, a private one." I cleared my throat.

"Kid, I told you she was bad." Duce spoke, reaching for another shot.

Waving my body guard over, I motioned for him to lead us to a private room.

"G5, show that nigga Jump Man P some love. He just signed a contract with us. That nigga sick as fuck on the court. We bringing home that trophy this year for sure." The DJ shouted me out.

Waving my hand at him, I followed Yssa to the private room.

"Two hundred dollars for a song." She spoke while twirling her hips.

I watched in awe as Yssa bounced her fat ass while City Girls, *Twerk*, blasted through the stereo. Her ass ate up the red g-string she wore as she popped each booty cheek in my lap. My hands went around her waist pulling her into my arms forcing her to straddle my lap. Running my thumb over the *Cherry* tattoo that was written across her shoulder blade surrounded by images of bring red cherries, I couldn't help but smile. The art work looked sexy as fuck pierced into her bright skin. On the other shoulder blade the name *Yassim* was written in big beautiful cursive lettering.

"You had a son." I asked, my eyes still trained on the tattoo.

"Yes." She looked down.

"Why you putting your head down ma?" Using my thumb, I lifted her head up by her chin until we were eye level.

"I'm sorry." She cried.

"Sorry for what?"

"For hurting you. I didn't mean to."

"Chill out ma, that was the past. We good." I assured her.

"You want another dance?" She asked wiping her tears.

"Do your thing, Cherry. I'm mad you got motherfuckers calling you by the nickname I gave you." I sucked my teeth.

"Well, you just gonna have to call me something else because these titties ain't little anymore." She winked removing her top allowing the perfect pair of breasts to bounce in my face.

"Damn." I groaned, groping them.

"Mm." She moaned rotating her hips on my lap.

"How you been tho?" I asked.

"Same ol' same ol."

"You still with that nigga Tommy?" I asked.

"He locked up now, but we still deal with each other from time to time." She rolled her eyes.

"What he do now?" I questioned.

"A gun charge and some other mess."

"You still dealing with bullshit I see." I scoffed.

"Really Pierre? I ain't got time for this; not with you, and especially not right now. You should know better than to come at me with some fuck shit." Hoping off my lap, she picked up her top and held her hand out.

Reaching in my pocket, I pulled out a knot of money and placed it in her hand.

"Thank you, best friend." She rolled her eyes before storming away.

Reaching for the bottle of Hennessey, I allowed my body to sink into the dark blue sectional before taking the bottle to the head.

Chapter Ten

YSSA

Seeing Pierre face to face after eight years did something to my soul. I've watched him play basketball on TV, owned his jersey, even rooted for him during the championship games, but nothing prepared me for actually being in the same room with him. He was the buzz on every sports channel, and everyone was talking about his contract with Miami. I knew he was moving back home. I just hadn't prepared myself for seeing him.

Life for me was just the same if not worse than it was eight years ago. With Tommy being in and out of jail. he was never on the streets long enough to make shit shake. The last time he got arrested we ended up getting evicted. Using the money I had saved up, I was able to cop me and my son a two bedroom apartment in the projects. It wasn't the best situation but I was managing. Neche, my neighbor who also had a son that was the same age as Yassim. introduced me to dancing at G5. Since we both were single mothers with bullshit ass baby daddies it didn't take much for us to click. Although I hated being friends with females, I needed her just as much as she needed me.

Peaking my head in Yassim's room, I walked over to his bed pulling the Roblox comforter over his body. Standing back, I admired my baby.

He was the only thing I did right in life. His face reminded me so much of his father it was scary. He was my light complexion but everything else was his father. Scanning his room, I picked up all of his toys, turned his PS4 console off and plugged in his lava lamp. My son was happy. I did what I had to do to make sure he had everything his little heart desired.

Even though we stayed in a high crime area that was infested with crack heads, the inside of our home was our domain. I kept our apartment cleaned, smelling nice and decked out with nothing but the flyest furniture and décor.

The knock at my door startled me. Neche was dancing so I know it wasn't her at my door. Reaching for my gun, I walked to the door holding it closely by my side. With all the break-ins and shit these crack heads were doing I stayed strapped.

"Who is it?!" I called out.

"It's me." They yelled back.

Peaking in the peephole, my eyes landed on Pierre. Sucking in a deep breath, I unlocked the door before pushing it open.

"What are you doing here?" I asked.

"Why you got that gun in your hand?" He rebutted, ignoring my question.

"You see where I live. Having a gun around these parts is essential."

"I feel you." He stepped around me into my apartment. "Same ol' neat freak." Pierre chuckled.

"Nothing changed, I'm the same ol' around the way girl. You the one that changed Mr. Big Money." I assessed eying down his assemble.

A Fendi shirt hugged Pierre's muscular frame, the jeans he wore slightly clung off his waist displaying the band of his Fendi briefs. On his feet was a pair of Fendi sneakers that matched his shirt perfectly. The diamonds he wore in his ears, around his neck and on his wrist threatened to start a blizzard, in the Florida's heat. That's how iced out he was.

Over the years, Pierre glowed up. He no longer had those pimples on his face. His skin was now smooth and rich like a Dove chocolate bar. His wild hair was now in dreads that were neatly twisted and styled going back. The huge gap in his mouth was now closed, and his teeth were white and perfect. With his skills on the court, millions in the bank and good looks, Pierre graced the cover of GQ and Forbes Magazine, covers I bought and kept tucked away.

"I know it." He chuckled. "I know you cooked something in here. I'm starving." He rubbed his stomach.

"You came all the way to the hood to eat?" I quizzed.

"I mean, the best food do come from the hood." He licked his lips.

"Yeah, I cooked." I headed to the kitchen with Pierre hot on my trail.

He took a seat at my small dining room table while I heated up a plate of baked spaghetti and fried fish with homemade garlic bread for him.

"You still baking your bread from scratch?" He asked when I sat the plate of food in front of him.

"You know it."

Pierre looked as if he wanted to say something but opted to shove the forked filled with spaghetti in his mouth instead.

"Lil man sleep?" He asked.

"Yup." I replied.

"How old is he now?"

"Seven."

"Why you being so short with me?

"I'm waiting for the lecture; I know it's coming." I crossed my hand over my chest.

"No lecture ma. You doing well for yourself considering the circumstances."

"How do you know where I live?" I eyed Pierre as he rose from the table and placed his plate in the sink. He was about to turn and leave the dish in the sink until I side-eyed him.

Reaching for the sponge, he added Dawn to it before scrubbing the plate clean.

"I have my ways." He responded once he was done.

Walking over to me, Pierre wrapped his hands around my waist. It felt good to be in his arms.

"Damn, you smell so good." He inhaled my skin. "You got so thick too." His large hands roamed all over my body.

The new Pierre was so confident, sexy, filled with so much swag. He was a lil arrogant but that shit was sexy on him.

"Yassim put a lot of weight on me. I tried to lose it all but this was the smallest I could get." I replied.

"I like this shit on you. You got some grown woman curves, enough meat for a real nigga." He huffed before planting kisses on my neck.

Sinking his teeth into my flesh, he sucked on my skin until I burned.

"Mmm." I moaned, enjoying the way his lips felt on me.

Turning my body around so that I was facing him, he sat me down on the counter pushing me down until my back was against the cool wood.

"I wonder if your pussy still taste sweet." He hummed, pulling my shorts off. "Damn, you got some pretty feet. You painted them shits white too. Oooo weee!!!" He joked.

"You play too much." I closed my legs, preparing to sit up.

"Stop playing, a nigga ready for something sweet." Pierre wedges my feet apart until I was in a split. Inhaling my juices, he licked my inner thighs, teasing me.

"Stop playing." I moaned.

"I spent eight years trying to push the feeling your pussy gave me out of my mind. I even fucked mad hoes trying to get over my first little heart break but I couldn't. This my pussy, I need my pussy. Can I have some of my pussy?" He licked his lips. Pierre's eyes mirrored the lust he was feeling.

"Yes daddy." I purred.

"Good." He plated a kiss on my pussy.

Pierre sucked on my pussy lips before finally using his tongue to penetrate me.

"Ahhh." I arched my back, searching for something to grab on. When I came up empty, I gripped on Pierre's dreads pulling him closer to me.

"Oh shit." I cried out in pleasure while he alternated between eating my pussy and my ass. When I would near my orgasm, he would stop and suck on my titties allowing my anticipation to build.

"Please."

"Please what?"

"Please make me cum." I begged.

"Why should I?"

"Because I love you." I answered truthfully.

Saying those words, releasing feelings I harbored for eight long years felt as if a weight was lifted off my shoulders.

"Fuck man." Pierre groaned.

Removing his long, fat black dick from his pants, he slid inside my girth with ease. Pierre strokes were slow but powerful. Wrapping my feet around his waist I pulled him in closer.

"I love you, too, ma. I've always loved you but you fucked me up." He confessed never missing a stroke.

"I know and I'm sorry."

"Shut up." He growled smacking me on the thigh.

Pierre made love to me until my toes curled and my pussy erupted then he flipped me over and fucked me until he was spraying his seeds on my back. From the kitchen counter to the bathroom we fucked all over my house. Now we were curled up in bed sharing a blunt.

"If I was your best friend, I want you around all the time, and I be your best friend if you promise you'll be mine." Pierre sung off key.

"You remember that song." Pierre asked, running his hand through my wild hair. Prior to our shower, it was nice and tamed now it was back to its curly state. Pierre loved my hair that way.

"Yup." I smiled thinking back to how tight we used to be.

"I'm sleepy as fuck, but I want my dick sucked first." He blew a cloud of smoke in the air.

Slithering down underneath the blanket, I gripped the base of his dick and began to put Supa Head to shame.

Chapter Eleven

PIERRE

"Bae are you listening to me?" My fiancé, Agaci asked.

She had just finalized her move from our house in Chicago to the mansion I purchased on Star Island. The month she spent in Chicago was the month I spent with Yssa. At first, I had every intention on resuming our friendship. I was with Agaci now and we were expecting our first child but that was easier said than done. All it took was one day, and I was back under Yssa's spell. The feeling I fought so hard to push away came rushing back. The fact that Tommy returned from jail didn't help much. Between Agaci being on my back and Tommy on hers we barely made time for each other.

"Yeah babe." I smiled looking over at her with a half-smile on my face.

"Are you ok?" She questioned.

"Yes, I'm fine." I rubbed her stomach.

Things between Agaci and I wasn't black and white. She was someone I started seeing my second year playing for Chicago. We weren't official; she was just somebody I could kick it and have sex with. When she told me she was pregnant with my baby, I had no choice but to make a honest woman out of her. Asking for her hand in marriage seemed like the right thing to do. Since I was a private person that flew under the radar the blogs new little to nothing about my personal life. I felt trapped in our relationship. I cared a lot for her but I didn't love her the way I loved Yssa. The only thing that kept me here was the fact that I didn't want to raise my son in a broken home. I wasn't raised that way.

"I want to get married before the baby is born." She rubbed her stomach. Agaci was now seven months pregnant but carried very small.

Agaci looked like Zonnique, Tiny's daughter. I remember seeing her and thinking that her bright skin and slim frame reminded me of Yssa. My attraction for her stemmed from the feelings I had for Yssa. Even though she broke my heart that night she told me she was pregnant for Tommy a part of me still loved her.

"Earth to Pierre!" Agaci snapped her fingers shifting my attention back to her.

"My fault. I thought you wanted to wait until after the baby's first birthday." I replied.

"I know but I really don't want our baby to be born out of wedlock."

"What's the difference? The both of you will have my last name." I stalled.

If I could push the wedding back some more I would. There was no way I wanted to rush into getting married.

"I know but..."

"But nothing. You're due in two months! There's no time to plan a wedding." I argued.

"There's plenty of time."

"I just think it'll be better after the baby is born. That way we can take our honeymoon on a private island as a family like we planned!"

"We can get married now, have a reception and sip and see after the baby born and still go on our honeymoon after the baby turns one, as planned."

"That makes no sense. Do you hear yourself? What the fuck is a sip and see?"

"It's like a party where people can come and see the baby." She replied as if that shit was normal.

"You see how these babies dying because motherfuckers with

herpes kissing all over them and shit. I'm not having no sip and see just to have a bunch of dirty ass people around my seed, nah. I know you ain't bring that shit up thinking it was cool." I shook my head.

"Can we at least talk about this, come to a compromise. You can't just say no and that be the end of it."

"When we get married, I want it to be carefully thought out and planned. I want it to be your dream wedding so you don't have to regret having a shot gun one. I want our child to be a part of our union. We talked about this but now you wanna rush the process. Why the sudden change?" I quizzed.

"You're right." She sighed.

"I know I am baby." I kissed her on the lips. Placing my hand on her small baby bump, I rubbed until my baby began to kick. We both agreed to wait until child birth to learn the sex of the baby.

"I'm ready to be Mrs. Pierre Blacksmith."

"I hear ya." Was my only response.

I should have been happy in this moment, in my fiancé's arms; however I couldn't stop my mind from wandering to Yssa.

Chapter Twelve

YSSA

"What are you doing here?" I asked, stepping to the side allowing Pierre entrance into our home.

"Wassup ma, you haven't been calling me. Talk to me mama." He demanded towering over me. Even dressed in something so simple as a pair of baller shorts and a white V-neck he was sexy as fuck. Tearing my gaze from his print that could be seen through the grey fabric, I shifted my weight from one leg to the other opening my mouth to speak but nothing would come out.

"Where Tommy at?" Pierre looked around.

"At the hospital."

"For what? He straight?" Pierre's voice was filled with concern. Even though the two wasn't as close as they used to be it was evident that they still cared for one another.

"Yup, he down there witnessing the birth of his daughter." I chuckled.

"Yo, are you serious right now. That nigga had a baby on you?"

"Two babies on me." I corrected him. "He has a son about the same age as Yassim. I know what you're going to say but save it." I held my hand up ceasing his thoughts that he was itching to voice.

Tommy was a fucked up ass nigga, I knew that. When Neche would tell me that I deserved better, I didn't believe her. I was just as fucked up as he was, and in my eyes we were meant for each other. I wasn't shit, he wasn't shit, we wasn't shit. Together we were content. For eight long years being with Tommy was all that I've known. He was my first real relationship, my adaptation of love. I clung on to him because in my mind I needed him. No matter what he did, I took him back, because having a piece of him was better than having no one at all.

"I just wished you could step out of your body for a quick second to see yourself how I see you. Why you putting up with that nigga ma? You too fly for that shit." Pierre closed the gap between us, draping his arm around my waist. "Damn, I missed you." His hands slid down my back side cuffing my booty cheeks from the bottom of my shorts. "Why you ain't been hitting me up." Pierre looked up at me.

The love he carried for me was visible through his eyes. His gaze was so intense that I had to look away.

"I've been working and..." Cupping my mouth, I ran to the bathroom. Flipping the toilet lid open I slid down to my knees and threw up everything.

"Ayo you good?" Pierre asked holding my hair back.

"Yeah I just been sick; it's the stomach flu." I lied.

Was pregnant with Pierre's baby; that's why I've been avoiding him.

Once I was done throwing up, I tried to stand to my feet but I felt dizzy.

"You good?" He asked.

"Yeah, I'm just a bit dizzy." I huffed, trying to regulate my breathing.

"I gotchu." Pierre assured me walking me to the sink. He helped me brush my teeth. How ironic that we stood in the bathroom, in the exact same spot I conceived our baby.

My mind traveled back to that night, one month ago. Pierre had my body pinned against the sink while he rammed his dick in me from the back. His fingers toyed with my clit while his dick massaged my g-spot. Clenching my pussy tightly around his dick he let out a moan and together we both came. It was the only time that night he didn't pull out.

"Here." Pierre handing me a bottle of water, snapping me out of my thoughts.

"Thanks." I twisted open the cap and gulped it down, thinking of the right way to tell him I was carrying his baby.

Before I could formulate a sentence with the proper words, the front door swung open, and there stood Tommy with a shocked expression on his face.

"My nigga, what's good kid?" He greeted Pierre dapping him up.

"Wassup fam, how you been." Pierre returned the love.

"Shit, I just been chillin'. You know how I do. Man I see you out here doing your thing. You sick as fuck on the court. I made a lot of money betting on you." Tommy eagerly spoke.

"Word? That's wassup."

"You know you gotta look out on some tickets for some of your games right.

"It's only right. I gotchu."

"What bring you around here?" Tommy looked from me to Pierre.

"I ran into Yssa and wanted to catch up with the both of you. A lot of time have passed and I didn't want to be back home harboring ill feelings. I wanted to personally come by and let you know all was forgiven." Pierre lied.

"That's wassup man, I appreciate that." Tommy pulled Pierre in for a brotherly hug. "That mean I'm invited to your wedding and shit?" Tommy chuckled.

Wedding? I thought feeling as if I was going to be sick again. Nothing in the blogs mentioned Pierre was engaged then again he was always the lowkey type.

"You know?" Pierre asked with a surprised look on his face. I could tell he wanted to turn my way and explain everything but he couldn't with Tommy standing in the room with us.

"Yeah, Ma Dukes filled me in when I went to visit her the other day. She told me about your lady and her expecting y'alls first child. She was going on about how we need to hurry up and kiss and make up in time for me to be your best man." Tommy chuckled.

I know what he was doing. He was purposely trying to put Pierre getting married out there to hurt me. The ringing of Pierre's phone put a pause to the conversation. Relief took over his body as he answered the caller on the Air Pods that were in his ears.

"Are you ok?" Pierre asked. "Alright, I'm on my way. Stop crying, ma, everything is going to be ok." He said before ending his call.

"Yssa, it was nice seeing you again... Tommy, I'll have to chop it up with you another time. Matter fact put your number in my phone." Pierre handed Tommy his iPhone XS.

"Hit me up fam." Tommy handed the phone back once his number was stored.

"I gotchu, y'all be easy." Pierre said before walking out of the house.

"Where's Yassim?" Tommy asked.

"He's with Neche; they went to the zoo."

WHAP!

Tommy slapped me hard across the face.

"You think I'm fucking stupid?" He yelled punching me with a closed fist.

"What the fuck are you talking about?" I cried cradling my nose that was now leaking blood.

"You fucked that nigga?" He asked getting in my face.

"What are you talking about?" I played dumb.

WHAP! WHAP!

He punched me two more times sending me in a daze.

"I bet your hoe ass fucked him. How much did you make huh hoe? I know you. Back then you didn't want him, now that nigga a famous basketball star you all on his dick?" Tommy snarled, kicking me in the back.

"Tommy stop; he's just my friend." I sobbed.

"Fuck you hoe. I don't trust your bitch ass!" Tommy angrily snapped as he continued attacking me.

My body began to grow weak with every blow and kick. I panicked thinking about the baby I was carrying. Even though I wasn't sure how Pierre was going to react, I made up my mind that I was going to keep my baby. Yassim brought me so much happiness that I was sure this new baby would be my rainbow after this terrible storm.

"Please stop." I whispered.

"Fuck you!" He yelled kicking me hard in the face. My head snapped back hitting the glass table hard before everything went black.

Chapter Thirteen

PIERRE

"Is everything ok with the baby?" I asked rushing by Agaci's side.

"Yes, my blood pressure is really high, so they want to keep me overnight to run a urine test. The doctors want to make sure there's not a lot of protein in my pee."

"Damn." I grabbed her hand, placing a kiss on her forehead. "My baby is good tho, right?"

"Yes, our baby is fine." She assured me.

"Good." I breathed out a sigh of relief.

Placing my head on the side of the bed, I tried to wrap my head around everything that just took place at Yssa's house. I knew without a doubt Tommy was purposely trying to throw me under the bus by bringing up my engagement. For the first time in his life, I was a threat to him. I was no longer the ugly duckling that had to be the third wheel. I was that nigga and he couldn't take that shit. In his mind he figured if he blasted me that would stop Yssa for fucking with me, but I hope that wouldn't be the case.

I wanted to tell her. I was going to. I just couldn't find the right words to say. I loved Yssa; she was my soulmate but that didn't change the fact that Agaci was carrying my baby. The entire situation had me feeling as if my life was a reality TV show.

"Baby, are you ok?" Agaci asked running her hands through my dreads.

When she did it, I felt nothing but when Yssa's fingers entwined my locs, I yearned for her touch. Since having Yssa back in my life I found myself comparing the two.

"Yeah, I just had a long day." I huffed.

My phone began to ring again. Looking down at it I realized it was a random number calling me. Hitting the ignore button I went back to my position just to get interrupted by the same caller.

"Hello?" I answered.

"Is this Pierre?"

"Yes, who is this?"

"This is Neche, Yssa's friend. I'm at the hospital with her. Tommy beat her up pretty bad. She wanted me to call you and asked if you can come see her." Neche spoke.

"Which hospital?"

"Broward General."

"I'm on my way." I replied hanging up.

"What's going on?" Agaci asked.

"I have something to handle real quick; call me the minute the doctor comes back, alright." I rushed out of the room not giving her the chance to reply.

Walking inside Yssa's room and seeing the condition she was in pissed me off. I knew Tommy was a fuck nigga but I didn't think he would go this damn far. Two black eyes decorated Yssa's swollen bruised face, her lips were busted and her nose looked as if it had been shifted. The more I studied her injuries the angrier I became. Kicking my shoes off, I got in the bed next to her, careful to not bump into any one her bruises.

"I'm so sorry." She sobbed looking up at me.

"What are you sorry for? This is not your fault." I soothed her.

"I lost the baby. I was going to tell you but then he came home." She blabbered.

"What baby?"

"Our baby." She confirmed. "I just found out I was pregnant. It wasn't Tommy's since the time frame didn't add up; he was still in jail when I conceived." She explained.

"Shit man! I'mma kill this nigga I swear!" I fumed.

"The police already picked him up, I pressed charges. I knew you would do anything to protect me but I couldn't allow you to risk your career that you worked so hard for in the process."

"I wish you would have allowed me to put hands on that nigga first." I grunted.

"Tommy was out on probation so he fucked himself up. Not only did he violate but this will be a new charge added to his long list of charges, his ass ain't getting out anytime soon." Yssa explained.

"What other damaged did he cause?" my eyes scanned her body looking for more bruises.

"Besides my face, I have a few bruised ribs . I had a mild concussion when I came in but I'm good now."

"Damn. I shouldn't have left you with that nigga, I should have known."

"You had to leave; your fiancé needed you. Is the baby ok?" She asked looking up at me with hurt in her eyes.

I wanted to tell you, I swear but I couldn't do it. All the feelings came rushing back. I fell back in love with you and I wasn't trying to mess that up.

"What about your fiancé? She's carrying your baby."

"I know man." I dropped her head. "On the real, I only proposed to her because I found out that she was carrying my baby. I don't really love her. I don't think I ever did. This may sound crazy but I only think I was infatuated with her because she somewhat reminded me of you." I chuckled.

The situation wasn't a laughing matter; however, I was sure my explanation sounded crazy as fuck.

"I have something to tell you but you have to promise me you won't get mad at me." Yssa nervously said.

"Talk to me baby." I turned to my side giving her my undivided attention.

"Yassim is your son." She blustered out knocking the wind out of me.

"What?" I frowned.

"Yassim, belongs to you." She repeated.

"I'm hearing what you're saying but how the fuck?"

"That night we had sex, I told you I was pregnant but I wasn't that night. I actually conceived our son."

"Why would you lie about some shit like that?"

"You was preparing to throw everything away for me. You started talking about putting school on hold so you could help me and I couldn't allow you to do that. If you would have stayed and waited on me you would have never been this superstar that you are now. I didn't want to hold you back, so I told you I was pregnant for Tommy because I knew that would break your heart enough for you to leave."

"That's some sick shit. When you realized you was carrying my baby, why didn't you contact me?"

"I didn't want to burden you. You were in college; the last thing I wanted to do was distract you with a baby."

"He's my baby tho!" I yelled. I felt like shit. Seven years of my son's life went by and I missed every single one.

"You had no right to keep that shit from me, that was foul as fuck! I would have come up with something; my mother would have helped. For seven years, you allowed my son to call another man daddy, the same man that snatched you away from me. You whack as fuck for that shit!" I yelled getting out of the bed, putting my shoes back on my feet. I had to get out of there before I started punching holes in the walls.

"I'm sorry Pierre." Yssa pleaded.

"Nah, sorry can't fix this shit!" I dragged my hands across my face. "Where is he?"

"He's in the cafeteria with Neche."

"Brody!" I called out for my body guard.

"What's good man?" Brody poked his head inside the room.

"I need you to get with whoever is in charge and have them arrange a private room for me, then I want you to go to the cafeteria and look for a woman name Neche, she's with a little boy. I need you to bring them to the room, let me know once everything is handled." I ordered.

"Yes sir." Brody nodded before backing away.

"Seven fucking years!" I yelled. "Seven!!" I knocked over a few medical supplies that were on the counter.

My chest began to tighten thinking about all the moments and memories I missed. Here I was a millionaire, a celebrity, living life while my son, my flesh and blood lived in the projects. Out of everything Yssa ever did to me this was something I didn't think I could forget.

"I just want you to get to know him; he deserved to know who his real father is."

"I had a right to know, I deserved that shit too! You know what? Shut the fuck up talking to me." I spat.

Looking Yssa in the eyes, her tears did little to move me. I loved this girl with all my heart, I gave her everything I had even when I didn't have much to give yet in return she continuously found ways to hurt me. I was disgusted with her, ashamed to be in love with someone so selfish. This was one act I wasn't sure if I could forgive.

"Everything is set up boss." Brody appeared in the room shifting me away from my thoughts.

Without uttering a word to Yssa, I walked out of the room.

"I want two guards securing this door at all times. Make sure you give her doctor my number and have them call me before she is released."

"Yes, sir."

I was boxed in by my security team as we walked through the corridors of the hospital. With a fitted cap pulled down low and a pair of shades, I walked with my head down in attempt to hide my identity. At this moment, the way I was feeling if approached by a fan the wrong way I would lash out, possibly tarnishing my image. When you're a celebrity, people assumed you didn't have feelings. It was frowned upon to display every day emotions. You have to be a robot that did and said the right things all the time.

"In here." Brody led me inside of a lounge.

"Neche." I approached the woman that sat with my son.

"I already know. I'll leave the two of you alone. If it's worth anything, all Yssa would talk about was how fucked up it felt keeping this secret from you. She really meant no harm, that girl really does love you." She spoke. With a sensual sway to her hips, she walked away before I had the chance to respond.

"Wassup man?" I took a seat across from Yassim, removing my hat and shades.

"Oh my God! You're Jump Man P! I can't believe this! You have to give me your autograph so my friends at school can have proof that I met you. Aww man I wished I had my mom's phone; we could have taken pictures." He beamed with excitement.

My words were caught in my throat as I studied his features. At a glance you couldn't see the resemblance; he looked more like his mother because of the complexion but if you really studied him against pictures of myself when I was his age there was no denying that we shared the same DNA.

"Can I have your autograph?" He asked again this time he reached in the center of the table for a pen and handed it to me. "I don't have any paper." He frowned. "Maybe the nurse can bring us some.

The oval sized birth mark on the side of his right hand near his pinky caught my attention. Bringing my right hand up to the table, I looked at the identical birth mark I had on mine.

I was in awe looking at my son, my first born child. Yassim was a handsome young man. His hair was long and thick just like mine. Yssa kept his hair braided going back into a man bun while the side neatly tapered into a fade. Both of his ears were pierced making him look like the ultimate pretty boy. Yassim's skin was nice and smooth just like his mother's, his teeth were perfectly white and straight with the exception of the small gap he had.

"Can I get a hug?" I asked.

"Heck yeah!" He jumped up.

Pulling my son into my arms, I felt a surge of energy rush through my body. This felt right, he felt like he belonged to me. This was my son. Now everything was starting to make sense; in the month that I spent with Yssa she always made sure he wasn't around. He was either asleep or with Neche. When I would bring him up in our conversation she would change the subject. I just figured she was doing that to protect my feelings when in actuality she was hiding the fact that he was my kid.

"I wish my mom was here; she loves you so much. We have matching jerseys of yours from when you played in Chicago. We don't have the Miami ones yet but I'm sure she'll get them. I'm a basketball player too. Well, I play with my friends but my mom says next season she'll sign me up to play for the city." He rambled on.

Just as I was about to open my mouth, the doctor walked in. I wanted to come out and tell Yassim that he was my son but I wanted to be sure first. While he was in the cafeteria I texted Brody with instructions to watch as the doctor swabbed his mouth; now it was my time to get swabbed.

"I'll be right back buddy." I assured Yassim.

"Are you going to get paper for my autograph?"

"Yup." I smiled at him.

Stepping outside, I followed the doctor into another room where he swabbed my mouth, placing the DNA sample in a bag.

"I need these results today, money is no issue, but you have to be positive that you can get them to me today. If not, I'll call around and find another lab."

"You have my word, I will personally do them for you." The doctor assured me.

"I just want to remind you that you signed a non-disclosure agreement, a word about this to anyone and your career will be over." I stated firmly while looking him in the eye.

"I take my job very seriously, you have my word that I will not speak of this to anyone."

"Good." I patted him on the back before walking away.

৯৯

"Yassim Jerrod Smith, is your son." The doctor said handing me the result sheet.

"Wow." I stared at the numbers in shock. "Thank you, doc."

"Anytime, is there anything else I can do for you?" He eagerly asked.

"I need you to check in on a patient for me, Yssa Smith, she's on the third-floor room 306. I want around the clock updates on her."

"Will do." He nodded.

"Thanks, I'll be sure to send you tickets to our first home game of the season, floor seats."

"Thank you so much, my son would love that!" His face lit up.

Walking back to the private room I've spent the last six hours in getting to know Yassim, I took a seat next to him.

"This is the best day, I swear!" His voiced was filled with excitement.

Since we were stuck in the room waiting on the results I had my security team bring up a bunch of board games, a TV, PS4, laptop, iPad, food and anything else Yassim requested. In the short time we've been together I learned that he was a very smart kid. He was even promoted to the third grade. He made all A's, he loved basketball, jammed to the Migos, and was addicted to Fort Nite. Although he wasn't growing up in the best environment Yassim was a great kid all around. Yssa really took great care of him, I was grateful for that.

"I have something to tell you; it's going to sound crazy but it's the truth." I spoke.

"What is it?" I asked.

"I'm your real father." I breathed out, anxiously waiting his reaction.

"Is that why the doctor swabbed my mouth earlier, for a DNA test?" He quizzed.

This kid reminded me so much of myself growing up; he was really smart. Advanced for his age. I really had to get him into a school that would cater to his academic needs.

"Yes."

"Is that why Tommy was always mean to my mom because he knew I wasn't his real son." He looked up at me with side eyes.

"How was Tommy being mean to your mom?"

"He would always yell at her, he was always nice to me but one time I heard him say it didn't matter if he had babies with other women because I wasn't really his son. I never said anything about it, I kept calling him dad because I wanted a dad but I knew he wasn't my real dad." Yassim uttered. His words ripped through my chest. My seed should have never had to feel that way.

"Well I'm here now and I'm your real dad. From this moment on I will always be here for you. Whatever you need, I'll provide." I assured him.

"What about Tommy?"

"You don't have to worry about him anymore."

"Can I call you dad?"

"According to this paper you can." I playfully punched him.

"Wow, my dad is a famous basketball player. Wait until my friends here this." I chuckled, slapping his hand against his forehead.

I didn't know where things would end up between me and Yssa or me and Agaci for that matter but one thing I knew for certain was that no one was going to get in the way of me creating a bond with my first-born son.

Chapter Fourteen

YSSA

"This is nice as fuck." Neche squealed as she walked through my new home.

It's been two months since Pierre found out Yassim was his son and he stepped up. The first thing he did was purchase a beautiful five bedroom, four and a half, two story beach house for me and Yassim. He upgraded my 2007 Nissan Altima to a 2019 Platinum Cadillac Escalade and the new Lamborghini truck. Since we wasn't talking much he wasn't sure which of the two I would prefer so he purchased them both. Yassim had everything his little heart desired, plus more. He had two rooms, one for all of his toys and gadgets and the other to sleep in. The indoor basketball was his favorite part of the house especially when Pierre was over.

Looking around my house, I couldn't believe how once again my life has changed dramatically. Not only did Pierre take care of Yassim, but he made sure I was good too, something he was not obligated to do. Despite him filling my bank account with more zeros than I knew what to do with, I was an authorized user on his black card; he wanted to be sure Yassim had access to anything he would need when he wasn't around. My bills were paid every month, my son was happy and I was happy that he was happy.

"Yeah, it's alright." I shrugged.

"What the fuck you mean, it's alright? This is everything!"

"To be honest, I'm happy that Yassim finally has his real father in his life that is, not only providing financially but is actually there being proactive. I just wish things were different. All this is materialistic shit, shit that when you die you can't take with you. Eight years ago, I would have been living my best life rolling in all this dough, but now I feel like I'm missing something. It just don't feel right." I sighed.

"Why because Pierre is with that hoe." She rolled her eyes.

"Yeah." I fumed.

"I say you beat her ass and go get your man back, I'm down with whatever." Neche jumped up into a fighting stance.

"Chile, I am not about to fight that girl." I waved her off. "They're engaged, she's at the hospital giving birth to his baby as we speak. Ain't no competing with that."

"Bitch! Have you looked around? This nigga is going above and beyond to take care of his son and it's because he wants to make sure you're good too. If he didn't still love you he would have went down to the courts, filed for joint custody and paid you child support every month. This nigga made you the authorize user of his credit card, he comes over here every day when he could just pick up his son and go. He's being stubborn right now but trust me he loves you just as much as you love him." Neche smacked her lips.

"I mean it is what it is tho." I shrugged my shoulders. "You staying over tonight?"

"Hell the fuck yes!" She beamed.

"Well make yourself comfortable, I'm about to take a shower." I said before making my way up the circular tiled stairs.

In my master bedroom, a room that was about two thousand square feet, I plopped down on the sectional that sat in the corner of my room. Since my room was so big I was able to section off an area decorating it as if it was a living room. I had more space in here than I knew what to do with so I just filled it up with furniture yet there was still a lot of room left.

Reaching for the picture me and Pierre took eight years ago, I laughed at how crazy we looked. We both looked at the camera making the silliest faces, but out of all our pictures this was my favorite one. That day I had just got done boosting, we'd went down to CiCi's Pizza and pigged out until I threw up due to over eating. I remember being mad that I got throw up all over my new Jordan's. Even though Pierre was trying to convince me that they could get cleaned I wasn't buying it. While I acted like a brat, he removed the shoes from my feet and cleaned them off. He then placed them back on my feet and carried me on his back on our walk back home. In front of his house, we'd stop and snap pictures on his phone. Pictures that captured us at our happiest time.

"Alexa! Play, One Last Cry."

"Playing, *One Last Cry* By Brian McKnight." Alexa replied before the soft croons of Brian's soulful voice filled my room.

Picking up my phone, I toyed with it wondering if I should text Pierre. He was here with Yassim earlier but had to cut his visit short when Agaci's mother called and told him that she had went into labor. I wanted to congratulate him on the baby but I didn't want to come off as being bitter. I wanted to tell him I loved him, fix things back to the way it used to be but part of me wouldn't allow me to. I was down to my last cry.

Chapter Fifteen

PIERRE

Pierre, I wanted to call you, but I couldn't bring myself to. I wanted to congratulate you on the baby, but I couldn't bring myself to do it. I'm happy for your new addition but I'd be lying if I said I was happy that you were marrying someone else. You said yourself, you only found Agaci attractive because she reminded you of me, but she's not me. There could only be one Yssa, one Cherry, one woman that held ownership of your heart and that woman is me.

Eight years ago when you wanted to be with me, I didn't blow you off because of your looks. I did because I felt like you were too good for me. In my mind, I hated the person I was so much that I purposely would set myself up for failure. A few weeks into my relationship with Tommy I knew he wasn't shit but I stayed because I felt like that was the only type of man I deserved. Now I know I'm worthy, now I know I'm capable, now I know my worth, now I know my place and it's with you.

I love you Pierre, I love you so much that it hurts me to know that I can't have you. Remember when I used to sing Sweet Lady, but I remixed it? Remember the words... Sweet Baby, would you be my sweet love for a life time, I'll be there when you need me.... I remixed it for you. You're my sweet baby, my Square, my soul mate... would you be my sweet love for a life time?

It's been two weeks since I've held this phone in my hand re-

reading the text Yssa sent me over and over again. Every time my fingers would brush across my keyboard with a response I would quickly delete it. Every time I would stand in the shower and rehearsed what I wanted to say, the moment the time came for me to say it I would chicken out. I was in a tight position, even if I was able to look past Yssa deceitful ways, Agaci had just given birth to my daughter two weeks ago. We were still engaged. My hands were tied, it was forced, and I was stuck.

Stepping out of the locker room, I left practice with plans on picking Yassim up but decided to head home first instead. I needed more time to get my thoughts together before approaching Yssa. I needed God to send me a sign, a miracle, something that would steer me in the right direction.

As I walked out of the door, my body guards swarmed me as I pushed past the slew of paparazzi that loitered around the arena praying to snap an image that would make them relevant. Stepping in my Wraith, I drove around the city, admiring how beautiful South Beach was before heading home.

When I walked in the house, it was quiet. That was odd because I noticed Agaci's mother car up front. Something told me to remove my shoes and creep in the house from the back, doing just that I neared voices that spoke in a hushed tone. I crept closer, being careful not to make a sound. When I was close enough I noticed the voices belonged to Agaci and her mother.

"You have to get him to marry you now." Agaci's mother said.

"We agreed to wait until the baby is a year old, Pierre is not budging." Agaci smacked her lips.

"Well make him budge! If he's back to seeing his ex you need leverage; you need to become his wife. If Persa was really his daughter then you would have had the baby as a golden meal ticket but since she doesn't belong to him your best bet is to get him to marry you. By doing that you can milk his bank account putting money to the side and if he does decide to leave you for that trash you'll cash out on a fat alimony check every month." Her mother replied causing my blood to boil.

"I can still get money from him for Persa. Pierre is a stand-up guy; he will make sure the baby is good."

"What happens when she grows up and look nothing like him, then what? For now, you're safe because she's still fresh and new but time is not on your side young lady; you need to move and move quick." Her mother ordered before the sound of her heels against the Italian flooring could be heard as she walked away.

"Oh Pierre you scared me." She jumped when she saw me standing there. "How was practice?" She asked, searching my eyes to see if I overheard anything.

"Practice went well. So, Agaci, when were you going to tell me that Persa didn't belong to me? On our honeymoon? Or after you and your thieving ass mama went down to the bank to *milk my account.*" I spoke in a calm tone. I was angry so I was trying not to react. I wanted to fuck both Agaci and her mother up but their money hungry ass would only use that as grounds for a law suit.

"Wh-what are you talking about?" She stuttered.

"Don't play stupid. I fucking heard everything! Yo! I swear all you bitches foul as fuck, so who the fuck does she belong to?" I seethed looking down at her with rage filled eyes.

"My ex."

"Don't say anything." Her mother sternly replied.

"You better say something! Speak!" I barked causing Agaci to jump. Tears trickled down her face as she trembled.

"When I met you, I had a moment of weakness and double back to my ex. I was already pregnant with his baby when we slept with each other." She explained.

"I swear you hoes are all the same. None of y'all asses can be trusted! Just to be on the safe side I'll have Persa tested. If she is not my daughter I want her last name changed immediately! In the meantime, you have ten minutes to grab as much shit as you can. I want you out of my fucking house. If you're not out in ten minutes Brody will forcefully remove you."

"Pierre, wait." Agaci cried out to me.

"Bitch fuck you!" I tossed over my shoulder before walking out of the door.

꧁

"I knew there was something off with that hoe the moment you brought her home to me. I just couldn't put my finger on it. I can't believe she tried to pin a baby on you just to con you into marrying her." My mother went off.

After learning that Persa wasn't my daughter, I packed up Yassim and took him to Atlanta with me to visit my mom. Out of all the women I've dealt with my mother was the only solid one.

"Well at least you gained one beautiful son. Yassim is amazing, I love him." My mother gushed.

"He's a great kid." I smiled.

"Wassup with you and his mother?" She questioned.

"Fu- I mean, forget her. She ain't no better than Agaci."

"Son, I can see it all over you are still in love with her."

"Ma." I dragged my hand across my face.

"Don't ma me. Answer me this... if Persa was your daughter and you wasn't with Agaci what would you guys set up be?"

"We would co-parent. I would pay her child support and organize days that I would keep her." I answered.

"So why aren't you doing that with Yssa?" She side-eyed me.

"Ma that don't mean nothing." I waved her off.

"It means everything. Pierre, I know you, you're the flesh of my flesh. Eight years ago I knew you had Yssa living in my damn house. I may have worked a lot but I never missed a beat. I never said anything because I trusted your judgement. I raised you to be a good man, I raised you to be respectful, helpful, caring, attentive, I raised you to be exactly how your father was. Back then I knew you loved her and I know you still love her, so what are you going to do about it?"

"I don't know." I truthfully replied.

꧁

"Dad, what's that?" Yassim asked as I flipped open and closed the black velvet box I held in my hand.

"Can you keep a secret?" I asked in a hush tone.

"Yup!" He beamed licking the ice cream from his cone.

"A long time ago me and mommy used to be really good friends, best friends. Well I loved your mommy more than a friend should but she wasn't ready. Eight years later I ran into your mom at a party, after seeing her for the first time after eight years the next day I called my jeweler and had him make this ring for her." I flipped open the box again to show him the engagement ring.

The custom made 12.65 carat octagon halo diamond ring shined brightly with clarity that could be spotted from miles away. The 18 karat white gold band was thick and drenched in diamonds. Inside, engraved in neat cursive lettering read... *Cherry & Square Forever.* The three hundred-thousand dollar ring was worth every dime I spent on it putting the twenty-thousand dollar ring I purchased for Agaci to shame. I ended up removing the diamonds in the ring that I took back for Agaci, turning them into earrings for Yassim.

"Are you going to give her the ring?" Yassim questioned.

"That's what I'm trying to figure out." I vented.

"I think you should."

"Why is that?"

"Well do you love mommy?"

"Yes, I love her a lot." I responded.

"She loves you too and when two people love each other they get married." He schooled me.

"Is that right?" I chuckled.

"Yup." He licked his lips.

My mini me.

"Let's finish up so I can take you home. Keep this conversation between us, ok?"

"I got it, dad."

After paying the bill for our dinner, we got in the car and headed in the direction of him and Yssa's house. When we arrived Yassim was fast asleep so I had to carry him to his room. Once he was tucked in, I backed out of the room leaving the door slightly ajar.

"Can I holla at you for a moment?" I pulled Yssa to the side.

"Wassup?" She asked fumbling with the bottom of her shorts.

"Next time you keep some life changing shit away from me I'mma break ya jaw." I playfully punched her on the side of the face. Gripping her by the jaw I pulled her towards me until our lips connected.

"You ain't gon do shit, Square." She joked pulling away from me.

"Why you always trying to play me?" I licked my lips hoisting her on top of the counter.

"I'm just stating facts." She moaned as I pulled her pants down.

"You right, you never have to worry about me putting hands on you, lying, cheating, or intentionally doing anything to hurt you. The only thing getting a beating is that pussy." I groped her womanhood causing her to shudder.

"Why are you doing this to me?" She moaned as I dipped my finger in and out of her honey pot. "What do you want from me?"

"I want you to be my wife." I stated before putting my mouth on her pussy.

Before she could say anything, I stuffed my tongue deep with her warm, wet, mound and slowly tongue fucked her.

"Ooouuu shit!!!" She cried out as I tripled her pleasure. With my tongue fucking her, I used one hand to play with her clit and the other to penetrate her ass.

"Fuuuuuuuuuuk!!" She called out rolling her hips.

While she was in her zone, enjoying the bliss, I discreetly pulled my hands away from her. I continued tongue fucking her as I reached in my pocket and removed the ring. Pulling my tongue out of her pussy I sucked on her clit until she came. As a powerful orgasm viciously ripped through her body like a category five hurricane catastrophically hitting land fall, I slipped the ring on her finger.

Pulling her body up until she was now sitting on the counter, I raised her hand that the ring sat beautifully on and began kissing her ring finger.

"Pierre what the fuck is that?" She screamed. Yssa eyes were wide as she stared at the ring in shock.

"You asked what I wanted from you, well I want you to be my wife. I already put the ring on your finger, all you gotta do is say yes." I cockily grinned.

The difference between today and eight years ago was my boost in confidence. I was that nigga and I knew that shit too.

"HELL TO THE MOTHERFUCKING YES!!!!!" She yelled in my ears.

"Alright, well bend that ass over so daddy can get some of that engaged pussy." I licked my lips.

Chapter Sixteen

YSSA

"Arrrrrrrgh!!!" I threw up everything I had for breakfast. When there wasn't anything else to throw up, clear liquid traveled up my throat and out my mouth

"You are a nervous wreck." Ms. Mary, Pierre's mom, said as she rubbed my back.

"Do you think it was those eggs we ate this morning; they did look a bit off." Neche chimed in.

"No." I answered, tearing myself away from the toilet seat, forcing myself up.

"I'm pregnant." I whispered.

"Come again?" Ms. Mary smiled.

"I'm pregnant. I took the test last week, confirmed with the doctor yesterday. I'm six weeks pregnant."

"Oh my God! This is amazing!!!" Ms. Mary squealed. "Why didn't that nappy headed son of mine tell me."

"He doesn't know." I said before swishing Listerine around in my mouth. "I want to be the one to tell him, so please, don't blurt it out before I get the chance to." I pleaded.

"It's your day." She winked, motioning for the make-up artist to start my make-up.

As I sat in the make-up chair that had the words *Soon to be bride...* neatly embroidered in the back, everything felt surreal. It took five months for the top wedding planner in Miami to execute my vision of a ball for my wedding. As a little girl, I was in love with the story Cinderella which was why I decided to go with the fairy tale theme.

"Bae!" Pierre's voice called out.

"It's bad luck to see the bride before the wedding." I yelled out.

"I know, I'm right here at the door. I won't come in. I have something to tell you." He said causing my heart rate to speed up. Thinking the worse, I feared he was calling the entire thing off.

"Uh-huh, I'm listening." I swallowed.

"Don't be mad at me, but I invited someone to the wedding and I would like for you to meet her before the ceremony starts."

"Pierre, if you brought some little groupie ass hoe up here to meet me thinking I get down like that you got me fucked up! This ain't TLC; I ain't on that Sisterwives bullshit." I snapped.

"Chill Cherry." He chuckled. "It ain't even like that witcho crazy ass. I'm about to send her in. Be nice or I'mma trip your ass when you make it to the alter."

"Shut up, Square, bye!" I giggled.

Shortly after, a lady walked in, dressed in a beautiful baby blue floor-length gown. She looked as if she could be in her early forties. She was a little on the thick size but her curves matched her frame perfectly. Her wild curly hair was pulled back from her beautiful face. It didn't take a rocket scientist to realize this gorgeous woman with my matching skin complexion was my mother.

"Hello everyone." Her soft voice greeted the entire room. "Hello Yssa." Her eyes landed on me.

Opening my mouth, the words refused to flow out causing me to clear my throat instead.

"Let's give them privacy." Ms. Mary smiled.

"I just want you to listen; you don't have to talk." My mother spoke.

Her voice was so beautiful, everything about her appearance was breathtaking. I wouldn't have even known she was homeless. The more

I look her over the more I began to get angry; if she was living so well why didn't she come back for me?

"My mother was a crackhead, and I never knew my father. Growing up, my mother would drag me to crack houses in search of her next hit. She didn't care that I was a minor and needing schooling; the monkey was on her back so bad that a hit was more important than me. When I was fourteen, I got into a relationship with one of her dealers. My mother was cracked out so she could no longer pay for her habits with her body so she used me instead. Denny, her dealer, was infatuated with me. Despite not eating most nights, I'd developed way too early sprouting curves that only a woman should have." She chuckled in attempt to fight back the tears that had now gathered in her eyes.

"With Denny, life was horrible. Although I had a roof over my head, food to eat and clothes on my back I was in an abusive relationship with a man that was old enough to be my father. When I couldn't do the things he wanted me to do because I was an inexperienced child he would slap me around. My mother turned a blind eye to everything because to her getting high was all that mattered. When I got pregnant with his baby, I ran away. I actually ran to social services and turned myself in but things only got worse." She sniffled.

"Once the state gained custody of me, I was placed in a foster home with other girls who were pregnant. Shortly after, I ended up losing that baby and was whisked away to another home where my foster father thought I was a tool for his sons. He had a son who in particular that showed signs of being gay. He would make his son have sex with me in attempt to pussy whip him straight, but that never happened. When I turned sixteen, I had enough, so I ran away and started living on the streets."

"I then met your father who at the time was homeless because his mother got deported back to the Dominican Republic. Your father wasn't fully Dominican tho; he was mixed. His father, your grandfather was Black. Just to let you know, you have a little bit of that Dominican blood running through your veins. Anyways, we both started living on the streets together. It was crazy because, despite not having a home to live in, we were in love and it was amazing."

"I ended up getting pregnant with you, and it was the happiest day of my life. We both tried to find jobs but due to us not having an education it was hard. I was able to get welfare, but that little bit wasn't enough to help. I wanted you so bad, I did, but I couldn't care for you. I remember one night sitting at this bus bench across from the church. The ladies there would feed me, bring me toiletry items, and they were very nice so when I had you I figured that was the safest place for you." The tears started to trickle down her face. Wiping them away she continued with her story.

"Giving you up was the hardest thing I had to do. I felt incomplete, so I turned to drugs. Your father tried to be there for me but eventually we drifted apart because of my habit. I then linked up with this pimp that I sold my soul in exchange for drugs. When my pimp got arrested on a murder charge, I ended up going down with him because I was in the car with him when they pulled him over and found the murder weapon. I spent four years behind bars because I needed his testimony to prove my innocence but his lawyer kept pushing back his trial date. Last year, I got released into a work release program where I spent six months before I was released back into the general population. I didn't know where I was going to go or what I was going to do until I met Pierre. He told me that he was in love with my daughter and that he was going to marry her. He wanted me to meet you but needed me to get myself together first. So he helped me get an apartment, car, and a job. I wanted to reach out to you so badly but he made me promise that I would get myself together first. He explained to me how you was a soft spot to him and he wouldn't allow me into your life until he was sure I was ready to be there."

"Well, I'm here and I'm sorry for any hurt and pain that I caused. I'm sorry if your life wasn't the best. I'm sorry that I wasn't there for you as I should have been." She cried. "Oh baby, don't cry on your wedding day. You're messing up your make- up." She chuckled through her tears.

It was too late. I was a mess as I sobbed. My make-up was already ruined as it ran down my face, dripping on my white satin robe staining the fabric.

"I forgive you." I choked out.

"Thank you baby." She wrapped her arms around me.

In a tight embrace, we rocked back and forth cleansing our souls, ridding our body of years filled with pain. It was as if the generational curse that had be placed on us had been broken. As we cried, my mother prayed and my body rejected every bit of the hurt I secretly held on to. When we pulled away from each other, we looked a mess but on the inside it was as if our soul had been reborn.

"Sorry to cut this short ladies but we have thirty minutes until go time." The wedding planner poke with her head into the room.

"You can send everyone back in."

"I should go." My mother said smoothing out her dress.

"No stay. You need a touch up." I held on to her. I felt like a little girl again afraid that she would leave and never come back.

&⚘

"Everything was beautiful." I smiled to Pierre who was now my husband.

"It better had been. I spent two million dollars on this wedding. I swear on everything I love I will kill you if you try to leave me." He gripped me by my chin before kissing me on the lips.

"Thank you." I looked up at him. My heart fluttered we he stared into my eyes with so much love. The way Pierre looked into my soul had me feeling all the love he carried for me.

"What you thanking me for woman?" He asked pulling me until I was sitting on his lap. "Damn this dress is huge." He laughed.

"Leave my Cinderella gown alone." I rolled my eyes. My luxurious beaded Cinderella dress was tight at the top and dramatically puffy at the bottom. The cathedral ball gown was amazing.

"Anyways, I wanted to thank you for looking out for my mother. Thank you for bringing her back to me." Tears trickled down my face.

"If you don't know this by now, understand that I will do anything to ensure your happiness."

"I love you Mr. Blacksmith."

"I love you more Mrs. Blacksmith." He licked his lips before pulling me in for a kiss.

The photographers we hired to capture our special day snapped pictures of us while our tongues danced with one another, lost into a passionate kiss as if we were the only ones in the room.

"At this time, if we could have the bride and groom in the middle of the dance floor so they can share their first dance together as husband and wife." The DJ called into the mic.

Our kiss went on for a little longer, causing the crowd that was filled with everyone from friends, family and celebrities to clap and cheer.

Leading me to the front under a huge carriage that was formed into an arch, smoke filled the dance floor as our DJ spun or first dance mix starting off with 50cent Ft Oliva, *Best Friend* remix.

"If I was your best friend, I want you around all the time." Pierre sung into my ear as we bounced to the song.

The song then switched to *Sweet Lady* by Tyrese, K- Ci & JoJo – *All My Life*, before Heatwave- *Always and Forever* bounced off the walls to the Versace Mansion, where our wedding was being held.

"When are you going to give me another baby?" Pierre asked while H-Town, Knockin the Boots crooned through the speakers.

"In about eight months." I replied placing his hands on my bells.

"Are you serious right now?" He took a step back from me to examine my belly.

"Yup." I giggled.

"That's why yo ass ain't been drinking." He chuckled.

"You got me. I wanted to tell you on our honeymoon but I had a feeling that your mama was going to let it accidentally slip."

"Yeah, her ass can't hold water for shit."

"Ain't that the truth." I agreed.

"You've made me the luckiest man on earth." Pierre held me tight in his arms, a place where I felt the safest. I could feel his love for me seeping from his pores covering me.

"Nah, the day you grabbed my shit up from that park and brought me to your house I knew then as long as I had you in my life I would always be the luckiest woman in the world."

Standing on my tippy toes, I pressed my lips into his as we shared a deep kiss to Jagged Edge- *I Gotta Be.*

EPILOGUE

Two year later...

Yssa

"Pierre, drop your arms around Yssa's waist... yes like that! Perfect!" The photographer directed as he snapped photos of us for the cover of Family magazine.

Since our big wedding two years ago, everyone has been contacting us for interviews and to be on the cover of their magazine. I was even able to be a part of the ESPY Awards where I presented my husband with the Best NBA Player award. Pierre was very discreet with his private life, especially his relationships; however, the day he proposed to me he made us public. Of course, Agaci tried to throw shade by calling me the homewrecking whore that stole her man, but Pierre shut that down quick letting social media know that I was his first and only love.

These last two years have been wonderful, hectic, yet perfect. I was now a mother of three, right after I gave birth to our son Yazz, I was pregnant six weeks later with our daughter Yasmine. Of course, Pierre wanted more babies, but I was looking forward to starting my journey as a business woman. Watching Pierre do his thing on the basketball court, with the many endorsements he was getting and the investments he was making motivated me to find my purpose outside of him and the kids.

A year ago, I opened my very first restaurant, Sweet Cherries. Business surpassed my expectation making my restaurant one of the number one spot in Miami that I was a few days away from the grand opening to my second location on Fort Lauderdale Beach.

"That's a wrap." The photographer announced snapping me out of my trance. "You guys have a beautiful family." He smiled at us.

"Thank you." I replied bouncing baby Yasmine who was getting really fussy.

"Let me get her." Pierre reached for his spoiled brat. At wo months, she was spoiled and it was because of him.

"There you go spoiling her again." I playfully rolled my eyes at him.

"I'mma always spoil my girls." He licked his lips before reaching in and pressing his lips against mine. "You are so beautiful." His eyes met mines causing butterflies to swarm in the pit of my stomach.

"Even with these?" I asked lifting my blouse to show him the tiger stripes I had all over my stomach.

"Hell yeah! Especially with those!! You carried three of my children for nine months and gave birth to them; if anything, those warrior stripes make you even more beautiful." He said before kissing me again.

"I'm still upset that you're going to miss my grand opening." I frowned. Pierre had an away game in Toronto.

"I know baby but I know you gonna do well. Daddy gonna make that shit up when we get home, I promise." He winked.

"You so nasty." I shook my head as we made our way to the car.

The moment we stepped outside paparazzi was in our faces trying to snap pictures. Although our security team did a wonderful job at keeping them away I still hated their asses. A few weeks ago, I was out eating with Neche, and I unexpectedly got my period and, when I stood up to leave, I had blood on my pants. Those fuckers had pictures of my blood stain pants all over the web within seconds. Pierre and his lawyers worked hard to get the images removed but that wasn't before the trolls all over the internet decided to come for me.

As Pierre drove us home, I couldn't help but to look back at my children. Yasmine was sleeping peacefully, Yazz was looking out the window with low eyes, and Yassim's head was buried in his phone while the music from his air pods flowed through his ears. He was an exceptional child, still making straight A's in school while taking after his father on the basketball court. There were days I found myself apologizing to him for allowing him to think that Tommy was his father.

I was glad Tommy was no longer an issue to us. With him violating his probation by beating me up he ended up having to serve ten years in prison. A year later he had another twenty-five years added to his sentence for the death of his cell mate.

Pulling up to the iron gate that secured our thirty million dollar, twelve bed, fourteen bath, two story waterfront Italian Estate, I couldn't help but to thank God. Every time I crossed the threshold of my home, I became grateful. Remembering the times when I didn't have shelter made me appreciate a roof over my head whether it was an apartment or an estate.

"What time you fly out tomorrow?" I asked Pierre as we made our way to the front door.

"Nine in the morning." He replied, keying in the door code.

"SURPRISE!!!" Everyone called out causing me to jump back.

"What is this?" I asked looking around.

"Since I won't be there to celebrate your grand opening with you I decided to throw you a party." Pierre beamed.

"Ouuu, you play too much." I fussed.

"You love me tho." He winked.

Looking around at the crowd of people, I spotted those that matter the most to me. Ten years ago, I was a lost soul, I had nothing to look forward to, no purpose, and no family. Since then I've gained a best friend that became my husband, three beautiful children, my mother and Neche the first female to ever become my good-good girlfriend.

"I love you too, Square." I kissed my husband.

At that moment, a powerful feeling rushed over me. Wrapping my arms tighter around my husband, my body fed off of his. He was truly my soul mate, my other half, my best friend.

The End.

SUBSCRIBE

Text Shan to 22828 to stay up to date with new releases, sneak peeks, contest, and more....

WANT TO BE A PART OF SHAN PRESENTS?

To submit your manuscript to Shan Presents, please send the first three chapters and synopsis to submissions@shanpresents.com

CPSIA information can be obtained
at www.ICGtesting.com
Printed in the USA
LVHW090332021019
632927LV00001BA/205/P